Eliza M. Rose was born in Dekalb, Illinois. At the age of 3, her parents moved her and her three brothers to Virginia Beach, Virginia. While growing up in Virginia Beach, Eliza held a special place in her heart for Illinois, especially the surrounding Chicago area. Currently, Eliza lives in Virginia Beach with husband, Brian, their children, and their family pets. She is on her 18th year as a public-school teacher. She has a Master's in Education and is working on a Ph.D. in Education. *A Tale of Prima Facie* is her debut novel and she plans to work on a second novel.

For my husband and the love of my life, Brian Bowhall.

Thank you for being my sounding board and support system.

Eliza M. Rose

A Tale of Prima Facie

Austin Macauley Publishers
LONDON · CAMBRIDGE · NEW YORK · SHARJAH

Copyright © Eliza M. Rose 2025

All rights reserved. No part of this publication may be reproduced, distributed, or transmitted in any form or by any means, including photocopying, recording, or other electronic or mechanical methods, without the prior written permission of the publisher, except in the case of brief quotations embodied in critical reviews and certain other non-commercial uses permitted by copyright law. For permission requests, write to the publisher.

Any person who commits any unauthorized act in relation to this publication may be liable to criminal prosecution and civil claims for damages.

This is a work of fiction. Names, characters, businesses, places, events, locales, and incidents are either the products of the author's imagination or used in a fictitious manner. Any resemblance to actual persons, living or dead, or actual events is purely coincidental.

Ordering Information
Quantity sales: Special discounts are available on quantity purchases by corporations, associations, and others. For details, contact the publisher at the address below.

Publisher's Cataloging-in-Publication data
Rose, Eliza M.
A Tale of Prima Facie

ISBN 9798891559622 (Paperback)
ISBN 9798891559639 (Hardback)
ISBN 9798891559646 (ePub e-book)

Library of Congress Control Number: 2025901474

www.austinmacauley.com/us

First Published 2025
Austin Macauley Publishers LLC
40 Wall Street, 33rd Floor, Suite 3302
New York, NY 10005
USA

mail-usa@austinmacauley.com
+1 (646) 5125767

Thank you to my husband, Brian, for encouraging and motivating me throughout the entire process. As a full-time educator, wife, and mother, I needed time to focus on bringing this narrative to life and my husband created space for that to happen. From cooking dinner, bringing our youngest to practice, and reading my manuscript, he supported me in so many ways. His feedback and encouragement alone motivated me to finish this novel.

The characters and events are not based on my childhood or life in any way. Thank you to my parents, Alan and Susan, for being loving and supportive. They have always been proactive and very involved in my life. When I was in first grade, my parents and teacher were concerned that I wasn't picking up on reading. It turned out that I had major vision issues which were corrected with glasses. From there, my mom spent hours teaching me how to read and write so I could catch up to my peers. I not only caught up but fell in love with reading and writing. My parents bought me my first mystery series and that has been my go-to genre ever since.

Thank you to the editorial and production team at Austin Macauley. Your expertise has been invaluable throughout this publishing journey.

Table of Contents

Present Day 6 October 2024   **13**

Bureau of Detectives, Forensic Services Division, Chicago, Illinois   *13*

5 October 1996 (12 Years Old)   **17**

Sycamore, Illinois   *17*

Present Day 8 October 2024   **23**

Trenton, TN   *23*

21 January 2006 (22 Years Old)   **31**

Chester, Illinois   *31*

Present Day 9 October 2024   **35**

Bureau of Detectives, Forensic Services Division Chicago, Illinois   *35*

New Year's Eve, 2015 (31 Years Old)   **38**

West Englewood, Chicago   *38*

Present Day 9 October 2024   **43**

Sullivan Maxwell's Apartment W. Madison St.   *43*

10 November 2016 (32 Years Old)   49

Bureau of Detectives, Forensic Services Division, Commander Forbes' Office   49

Present Day 9 October 2024   54

Aurora, Illinois   54

New Year's Eve, 2016 (32 Years Old)   60

Downtown Chicago   60

Present Day 10 October 2024   68

Bureau of Detectives, Forensic Services Division   68

14 January 2017 (32 Years Old)   74

Bartlett Cemetery Bartlett, Illinois   74

Present Day 10 October 2024   78

Sycamore, Illinois   78

8 June 2002 (18 Years Old)   89

Sycamore, Illinois Graduation Day   89

Present Day 11 October 2024   96

Sully's Read n Sip W. Madison St.   96

Thanksgiving Day, 2008 (24 Years Old)   103

Sycamore, Illinois   103

Present Day 11 October 2024   107

Bureau of Detectives, Forensic Services Division   107

12 July 2013 (29 Years Old)   112

My Apartment N. Clark St.   112

Present Day 11 October 2024	**115**
Aurora, Illinois	*115*
4 October 2013 (29 Years Old)	**123**
Schaumburg, Illinois	*123*
Present Day 12 October 2024	**127**
Sully's Read n Sip W. Madison St.	*127*
14 October 2013 (29 Years Old)	**131**
My Apartment N. Clark St.	*131*
Present Day 12 October 2024	**133**
Bureau of Detectives, Forensic Services Division	*133*
10 March 2014 (30 Years Old)	**141**
The Bean Chicago, Illinois	*141*
Present Day 12 October 2024	**145**
My Apartment N. Clark St.	*145*
9 March 2003	**152**

Present Day
6 October 2024

Bureau of Detectives, Forensic Services Division, Chicago, Illinois

Thump, thump, thump.

My eyes spring open. There's a familiar aching sensation in my lower back and neck as I sit up, feeling disoriented, trying to catch my bearings. Stretching my arms overhead and rolling my neck from side to side gives little reprieve to my sore joints.

Soon, the brain fog begins to clear and I slowly recognize my surroundings, bare white-washed walls, two rickety wooden chairs, an L-shaped desk covered in disorganized piles of paperwork.

Thump, thump, thump.

I rub the sleep from my stinging eyes and wipe the drool from my mouth with my sleeve. Straightening my back in my chair while running my hands haphazardly through my hair, I manage to clear my throat.

"Ahem. Come in!" My voice nearly gives out on me.

The office door opens slightly. A familiar face peers in. His blue, deep-set eyes meet mine and I look away.

"I'm not gonna lie. You're looking rough," Ezra says with a smirk as he obliges himself to take a seat. He smells of cedar aftershave. I suppress my envy as I glance at his freshly ironed clothes and well-rested appearance.

"Yeah, well, I didn't sleep last night," I retort while tapping a pen on my desk impatiently.

I'm sure he could care less about my personal battles with insomnia. It's then that I notice a case file in his hands. He knows I've spotted it, so he sets it down on the chair next to him. His eyes meet mine. *What game is he playing?*

"I suppose you're too exhausted to look into the latest case then," Ezra taunts and then begins to stand.

"You know, no matter how you feel about me, I am your superior. Hand over the case file," I demand. My voice has surprisingly regained its authoritative tone.

Ezra scoops up the file from the chair beside him and in one fell swoop, slides it across my desk and walks out, allowing the door to slam behind him.

The vibrations cause my name plate to fall from my desk. I stand, struggling to overcome the sharp pain shooting from my lower back to every appendage, and walk unsteadily to pick it up. After replacing it, I stand back to briefly admire it. *Commander Mila Taylor.*

After settling back in my chair, I open the top desk drawer and take out a hand mirror. Ezra wasn't kidding. I hardly recognize the person staring back at me. My hazel eyes, which were once a feature to be admired, are overshadowed by the dark circles surrounding them.

My fair complexion appears almost ghost-like from all the hours spent indoors working on cases, leaving little time to enjoy the sunlight. I'm the depiction of a walking nightmare. I poke at the tender area under my eyes and consider covering my insecurities with makeup, but instead, return the mirror to the drawer and slide it closed.

I gingerly open the case file. Trying to shake my shortcomings of sleepless nights and falling asleep while on the job, I delve into my newest quest to put another killer behind bars.

At first glance, the file appears to contain the classic ingredients of a would-be cold case. Thirty-two-year-old Caucasian male, Sullivan Maxwell, bachelor, never married. Cause of death, strangulation. Pronounced dead in his apartment on the Near West Side.

No leads and limited evidence, a print lifted off a mug. The print didn't belong to Sullivan and it isn't a match to anyone in the criminal or civil databases. For all we know, Sullivan could've just invited a neighbor over for a friendly cup of coffee.

The detective at the scene, Ezra Wilkins, interviewed the neighbors and the doorman. Both claim the man had no social life, no love interests, and invested all of his time in his second-hand bookstore and coffee shop, *Sully's Read n Sip* on W. Madison St.

This guy sounds similar to me, minus the death by strangulation part. Just an introverted guy invested in his passion. Too invested to have many social ties.

My eyes glaze over as I look at the graphic crime scene photos. In my early years on the job, I had struggled to look and even found myself vomiting in the bathroom afterwards.

Now, several years in, I'm just analyzing evidence, searching for leads hiding within the glossy images. Flipping the folder closed, I rub my eyes, attempting to refocus my vision.

I didn't always want to be a detective. Having barely known my mother and having been raised by an uninvested father, I've never been the nurturing type either. I never dreamed about being a doctor, a veterinarian, or a teacher like many of my peers.

Until age twelve, I really didn't know what was to become of me. For most, there's one significant event that sets them on the trajectory toward their destiny. Mine was witnessing the murder of my older sister.

5 October 1996
(12 Years Old)

Sycamore, Illinois

Dad's station wagon is gone and my sister is in the middle of third period. I sprint across the lawn and hurriedly look around before inserting my key into the front door. After locking the deadbolt behind me, I stand in the entryway, catching my breath.

I exhale a sigh of relief as I fling my backpack to the floor. The adrenaline is wearing off. Now, I have to calm my nerves and make the most of my fleeting, newfound freedom.

I have it all planned. Dad and I usually get home around the same time, about 4:30. Farah is working a shift at the skating rink after school, so we won't expect her home until at least 8.

I'll just relax around here until quarter after 4. Then, I'll take a walk around the block, making it look like I'm walking home from the bus stop just as Dad pulls into the driveway. I can't help but smile at the fact that I'm actually pulling this off. I can envision myself doing this regularly.

School is for some, but not for all. Most certainly not for me. I'm not failing but I'm not flourishing either. There are no subjects or extracurriculars that particularly interest me. I don't have a friend group that I look forward to seeing in the hallways or giddily pass notes with during class.

On the same token, I'm not a troublemaker either. I just exist in space and time. Some teachers notice me and attempt to take interest, but since I'm not failing any classes, most just float me along to the next year, the next teacher.

That's why I chose to break free today. I rode the bus to school but instead of allowing myself to be ushered into the double doors of my middle school nightmare, I veered left and headed back home on foot. Miraculously, no one saw me. No one stopped me, in the same way that I didn't stop him.

In our room, I fling myself onto the bottom bunk and while contemplating taking a nap, stare at the wooden planks holding Farah's mattress above me. Farah's a good sister given the circumstances. I was only two when Mom died, but being four years older, it affected Farah a great deal more.

Our mom had been diagnosed with lung cancer shortly after I was born. I was often left in my crib for hours on end. Most days, Mom was too weak to get out of bed and Dad was either working or passed out on the couch with a hangover.

Despite being a small child herself, Farah would check on me while in the crib. She told me she would talk to me through the bars even when I couldn't understand her. I'm convinced that Farah is the only reason I survived.

She gave me the human contact I needed to thrive and grow into a fairly normal child. After Mom succumbed to cancer, Farah held onto a lot of resentment toward Dad for not being able to hold a job long enough to provide our mom with the quality treatments that might've saved her life.

Relatives defended him and said he had done all he could, but Farah was never convinced of that. Their relationship has been strained ever since.

To add insult to injury, Dad makes her turn her entire paycheck over to him to help with the bills. As soon as I'm old enough to work, he'll make me do the same. Right now, I'm responsible for making sure dinner is on the table each night.

I'm an awful cook but with a little extra salt and pepper, anyone can choke it down. Dad doesn't complain because most of his diet consists of cheap whiskey and beer anyway. Farah eats at the skating rink before coming home, so I'm mostly just cooking for me and to stay in Dad's good graces.

The familiar sound of a key rattling in the door awakens me.

I overslept! What time is it?

I squint to look at the alarm clock on the dresser. It's only 3. I dash over to our window and gently peek through the blinds. Dad's beat up station wagon is in the driveway.

Why is he home?

I hold my breath. Hearing footsteps echoing through the house, followed by the fridge opening, I creep toward the bedroom closet and slip inside. A bottle cap hits the kitchen floor. I realize I'm still holding my breath, so I gently exhale.

This was not in the plan. My hope is that after a couple drinks, he passes out in his recliner. I can sneak out and re-enter like nothing ever happened. The front door creaks open. Soft footsteps make their way through the entryway and into the living room.

"What are you doing? Why aren't you at work?" Dad barks from the kitchen.

"Dad, I told you this already. I put in my two weeks at the skating rink. My grades are suffering. I can't work like this every day. I need to focus on applying to colleges and getting scholarships." Farah sounds exasperated.

This conversation is news to me but it sounds like Farah has brought this up to Dad many times before. I sense the frustration in her voice.

"You're going to the skating rink to beg for your job back." Dad's voice sounds like it's coming from the living room now.

"No, I'm not," Farah unwaveringly rebuttals. I've always admired her strong will, but she's flirting with danger right now.

Farah, please just leave and pretend like you're going to do what Dad says.

"I'm not going to warn you again, Farah. Go get your job back or I'll drag you there myself." Dad's voice sounds closer, which means he's moving in Farah's direction.

Farah stands her ground with a firm, "No."

I hear scuffling and grunting as Farah's keys drop and clang against the floor. I imagine Dad has grabbed hold of her and is attempting to drag her toward the front door. Farah is strong, probably stronger than anticipated.

I imagine her heels dug into the ground, resisting his firm grasp and forceful pull. I will never forget what followed. The struggle ended with the sickening sound of the bottle slamming into Farah's head and the thump of her lifeless body falling to the ground.

Later, I'd find out that a combination of the blunt force and close proximity of the bottle hitting her right temple caused traumatic brain injury.

Realizing what he's done, Dad drops down to the floor and cries out in agony, "Farah? Farah, I'm sorry. Wake up!"

I'm frozen in the closet, not breathing again. It sounds like he's shaking Farah, as if he doesn't believe she's truly dead. That he murdered his daughter over a paycheck. Suddenly, there's deafening silence.

What's happening? Why is it so quiet?

When I finally hear movement again, it sounds like Dad is walking toward the front door. He's picking something up.

My backpack!

I leap out of the closet and lock the bedroom door. "Mila?" Dad shouts as he's banging on the door.

I yank the blinds open and climb onto the dresser to open the bedroom window. As soon as my feet hit the ground, I run. I run like my life depends on it.

When I arrive at the precinct, I'm shaking, sweating, and in utter shock and disbelief. I throw up on the front steps before entering. Not realizing at the time that I was entering my destiny.

Present Day
8 October 2024

Trenton, TN

The driver pulls up to the one-story brick, ranch-style home. As I stand on the sidewalk admiring the quaint characteristics of the house, my cell vibrates. It's Ezra.

"Hello," I answer sharply.

"Where are you?" Ezra never wastes any time with small talk.

"On the sidewalk, in front of Sullivan's parents' house. Why? What's going on?" I pretend not to notice the annoyance in his tone.

"You're interviewing the next of kin without backup?" *I'm not sure why he sounds shocked by this. He's known me long enough to know that I prefer to work alone.*

"Don't you think you're overstepping your authority, Detective?" I challenge his question with a question.

"Don't you think you're breaching protocol, Commander?" *Again, why is he suddenly surprised by this?*

"I have a recorder and will be sure to turn in the evidence upon my return." I'm confident that this response will be enough to finally shut him up. I can't help but smile when it does.

There's silence between us.

"Have you been to the crime scene?" Ezra finally breaks the silence.

"You know that's not my style. Besides, the crime scene has already been processed by one of my best detectives." Since no solid evidence was found at the crime scene, Ezra most likely took this as a backhanded compliment.

He releases a deep breath of discontentment before conceding, "I look forward to reviewing the evidence then."

"Oh and Wilkins?" The fake sweetness is dripping from my voice.

"Yeah," he responds in a most disinterested manner.

I adjust to a more assertive tone. "See to it that the autopsy report is on my desk. We need to start looking for a potential murder weapon."

"Sure thing," he replies, yet I can sense his sarcasm.

"Good day, Detective Wilkins."

As I hang up, I acknowledge the true intentions behind Ezra's call. He's heckling me, knowing very well the kind of detective I am. The kind who doesn't ask for permission or forgiveness. He knew his obnoxious phone call would only perturb me rather than deter me.

To regain composure, I fix the button and the collar on my navy blazer. Between the flight, checking into my hotel, and the drive here, I didn't have time to iron out the creases in my pants suit. This will have to do.

Sullivan's parents agreed to speak with me and I couldn't afford to give them time to change their minds.

Two days into the case and still no leads. I'm banking on this interview to point us in the right direction.

As I walk up the driveway, I stop to check my appearance in the reflection of a tinted sedan. My stringy, shoulder length hair makes my face appear longer than it actually is. I smooth down an auburn flyaway and look away in disgust. *I need a spa day after this.*

"Thank you for agreeing to meet with me, Mr. and Mrs. Maxwell. Please accept my deepest condolences for the loss of your son." I look around and observe family photos hanging nearby on the living room walls. Primarily photos of Sullivan at different stages in life, infancy, adolescence, high school graduation. By the looks of it, he's an only child.

Mrs. Maxwell, a frail woman in her mid-60s, wearing a pink floral print top and blue jeans, nods as she sits across from me. Her bottom lip is quivering as she holds back tears. It's apparent that I'm going to have to rely on Mr. Maxwell to answer my questions.

"May I?" I direct the question to Mr. Maxwell as I pull a small recording device out of my bag. He nods in agreement. I proceed to take out a small leather-bound notebook and lay it neatly on my lap.

The fine tip ballpoint pen tucked within the pages. After pressing record, I open the notebook to a blank page and prepare to take notes.

As I open my mouth to speak, I sense it's already too much for Mrs. Maxwell. Before I can release another syllable, she stands unexpectedly. She manages an apologetic, "Excuse me," as she rushes out of the room, presumably toward her bedroom.

Mr. Maxwell clears his throat. "Please have compassion on her, Detective, and allow the interview to continue with just me. Sully is—was our only child."

A tear rolls down his cheek and he doesn't bother to wipe it away. "This is the most unthinkable, unbearable pain imaginable."

"Of course. Just to make sure it's on the record, you agreed to this interview. I'm not forcing you or Mrs. Maxwell to participate. Do you still want to proceed?" I inadvertently hold my breath while awaiting his response.

"Yes, yes, we need to continue. I need to continue. We need closure for our Sully boy."

Calling a thirty-two-year-old man 'boy' seems odd but I don't draw attention to this observation. This is obviously an extremely tight-knit family. I'm sure Sully was spoiled being an only child, not necessarily with money but with attention.

"Thank you, Mr. Maxwell. Please begin by describing Sullivan's childhood. The more you can tell me about him, the easier it is to pick up on leads." I allow my body to relax now that the interview is officially underway.

"As a boy, Sully was even-tempered and content. He was always looking for ways to help me and his mom. We were in awe of how such a big heart fit into such a little body. Now, don't get me wrong."

"He wasn't always the perfect angel. I mean, he got himself into his share of trouble when he was an adolescent. Testing the waters, pushing the envelope, like most teenagers do." Mr. Maxwell paused when he saw my eyebrows rise.

"Trouble? Like what kind of trouble?"

"Oh no, nothing like what you're thinking. Just the typical teenage kid stuff like pretending to do his chores so he could play video games. There was one time the sheriff brought him home because he decided to skip school and was caught reading a book at the local library. He wasn't a very good troublemaker. Who skips school and goes to the library?"

Mr. Maxwell chortles. I can see his mind escaping to memories of Sully's adolescent years. I smile faintly and move on to my next question.

"Let's fast forward to after high school. What were his plans? His goals?"

"Sully loved to read and wanted to open his own second-hand bookstore and coffee shop. He was accepted to Northern Illinois University and four years later, graduated with a business degree."

"Why NIU?" *If he was so content, why did he want to go so far away?*

Mr. Maxwell senses what I'm thinking. "His mother and I wondered the same thing. We had no idea that he wanted to move north and were equally shocked when he decided to open his shop in downtown Chicago."

"The fast-paced city life was such a contradiction to his easy-going, introverted personality. We didn't argue with him though. He was our boy and we wanted the moon and the stars for him, so naturally, we supported him through it all. Even gave him the money he needed to close on the store."

"Did a love interest lead him to NIU or to downtown Chicago perhaps?" So far, this interview hasn't presented any persons of interest. I need to dig deeper.

"While at NIU, Sully told us about a date here or there, but he always found a flaw that prevented a second date. He was looking for someone with the potential to follow his dreams with him but he said most of the girls his age were focused on superficial things."

"He did find a best friend though. A nice young man named Davis Parks. We spent some time with him when we'd visit. They were dorm mates freshman year, shared an apartment through senior year, and then moved to Chicago to open the shop together."

Now, we're getting somewhere. I scribble NIU and Davis Parks in my notebook.

"Do you have a phone number for Davis Parks?" I inquire hopefully.

"Sadly, no. While in Chicago, Davis met a girl and eventually got engaged. He felt like the shop was just a school-boy pipe dream and too much of a financial burden. It was fine when it was just him and Sully but now, he was preparing to start a family."

"Davis urged Sully to sell the shop. Sully was heartbroken but let Davis out by buying his half of the business from him. They went their separate ways. They've only spoken once, maybe twice, over the last eight years."

"This is still worth looking into. I'll see what my team can uncover about Davis. It's important to know the last time they spoke."

For the next twenty minutes, Mr. Maxwell tells me all the mundane details of Sullivan Maxwell's personal and professional life. Some of which I already know just from reading the case file.

He spent all of his time at his shop, either working or reading books. He had a small staff of three employees. I jotted their names down in my notebook.

He visited his parents twice a year, for Christmas and for a week over the summer. His parents visited him on occasion but travel was becoming more and more taxing on their aging bodies.

I prepare to wrap up the interview, when Mr. Maxwell brings his hand to his forehead and gasps, "How did I forget? There was a woman, well, sort of. I don't know if he met her in person before he—well, anyway. She didn't live in Chicago."

"They met online about 6 months ago. Sully wasn't very forthright about sharing information about her with us. We wondered if he was embarrassed that they met online. That we might not consider it a real relationship."

"Did he give a name?" I lean forward in my chair.

"Natasha? No. Natalie? No. I've got it." Mr. Maxwell snaps his fingers. "Natalia. No last name though. I'm sorry. This isn't very helpful."

"I have more information now than when I arrived, so everything you've shared is helpful." I press stop on the recorder and reach out to shake Mr. Maxwell's hand. "Thank you again for meeting with me. Trust me. I'll bring you and your wife closure." Mr. Maxwell shakes my hand firmly.

Once outside, my lungs feel lighter as they take in the fresh air. While I'm not one to break a sweat under pressure, interviews always feel stifling. The length of time it takes to uncover one, maybe two, useful pieces of information is frustrating to say the least.

After all these years, I struggle with patience. I will the system to move at a faster pace but that's not real life. Even with my dad's case, my testimony wasn't enough for him to be found guilty without a lengthy trial.

Since I overheard the incident and wasn't an eyewitness, it allowed for a degree of reasonable doubt. The trial was drawn out further when his lawyer pled not guilty by reason of insanity.

21 January 2006
(22 Years Old)

Chester, Illinois

This is the account of the first time and last time I visited my father. After a forensic psychiatric evaluation diagnosed him with dissociative identity disorder, the court had no choice but to commit him to a maximum-security mental institution.

The whole thing made me sick. Even at the age of 12, I recognized that this man had gotten away with a crime. Rather than being convicted and thrown in a prison cell to rot for the rest of his life, he was a patient in a mental hospital.

The only consolation was the rest of his life was drawing near and that's the only reason why I'm visiting him today. I sign in at the front desk and hand my identification to the receptionist.

"Please stop by before leaving to pick up your ID," the receptionist says without looking at me.

I don't blame her. I'm sure this job was not within her top five aspirations growing up. In the waiting room, a seat near the window looks inviting, so I sit down and stare out the window as I wait. Not much of a view, just a line of greenery and foliage, but it's enough to allow my mind to wander as I wait.

Click. I look up to see the heavy door leading to the visiting area slowly opening. "Taylor," a male nurse with a husky voice calls out. He looks more like a bouncer dressed in scrubs. Being a maximum-security facility, housing mentally ill men, petite female nurses are probably out of the question, I reason.

I follow a couple feet behind the nurse as he leads me down an empty corridor and through another heavy, metal door. In an open, well-lit room, he gestures toward one of two tables bolted to the floor.

On either side of the table, there stands a chair bolted to the floor. Barred windows on one side of the room allow just enough light in. The white-washed walls are bare.

All are precautions to prevent the patients from using their surroundings to harm themselves or others during visits. To most, the scene would be eerie and unsettling. To me, it was just like entering a chapter from my textbook on criminology.

I'm in my fourth year of my bachelor's degree in criminal justice. That fateful day in 1996, gave my life purpose. Despite being thrown into the foster care system, I managed to make it through high school with a decent GPA.

You'd be surprised at how many universities took pity on me after reading my admissions essay, offering full rides with a little extra for housing and books. From here, I'll join the police academy with the end goal of eventually being promoted to the Detective's Bureau.

I adjust my position in the cold, hard seat several times as I wait for the patient to be brought out. Another *click*, and I look over as a heavy door leading to the patient quarters slowly opens.

I hardly recognize this man shuffling toward me. His once thick, dark hair is gray and thin. He's skin and bones. Sunken cheeks and dark circles under his eyes betray how ill he truly is, not just mentally but physically.

"Telling you I'm dying is the only way to get my beloved daughter to visit, heh?" Dad says as he slides into the seat across from me.

I remain stoic with my hands folded on the table. I refuse to react, to give him the satisfaction of getting a rise out of me. "You really are sick." I shake my head.

"After all these years, don't tell me, you don't believe why I'm here. Have you read any of my letters?"

"Is this what you want to talk about? The letters I haven't read? The lies I haven't indulged? Tell me why you asked me here or I'm leaving now." I move slightly as if I'm ready to stand up and advance toward the exit.

"Ok, ok." He raises both hands mid-way in an act of surrender. "I have 5 months to get my affairs in order. At least, that's what the doctors say. I have some savings in an account and I want you to have it. Do you have something to write with? I can give you the account information."

"Seriously?" I stand up. "I don't want your money. I've done well enough without it. You could've just told me this over the phone and saved me the drive."

"Please, sit down," Dad begs. "That's not it. There's more."

I sit but my legs stay slightly turned, in preparation to stand again.

"Go on," I demand. At this point, I'm visibly agitated. I feel flush and resent him for evoking this reaction from me.

"I really need you to read the letters I sent. They explain so much. You don't owe me anything, but you do owe it to yourself to read them. You'll see things in a different light, I promise."

I stare at him in silence, waiting for him to continue. He closes his eyes and rubs his temples, then proceeds, "I'm trying to protect you, Mila. To save you."

"Oh yeah? To save me from what?" I snort and lean back with my arms crossed.

His eyes burn into mine as he says, "To save you from yourself."

Present Day
9 October 2024

Bureau of Detectives, Forensic Services Division Chicago, Illinois

As requested, the autopsy report lay like a present waiting to be unwrapped on my desk. The toxicology report shows no sign of foreign substances in the victim's bloodstream. There was no blunt force trauma.

Sullivan was a petite man, 5'5, a meek 140 pounds. It wasn't necessary to beat or drug him to overpower him. The bruising and lacerations on his neck were caused by a 20-inch heavy duty zip tie.

Its whereabouts are yet to be discovered. Unless the killer is clumsy, the zip tie will never be recovered. This is one of the easiest murder weapons to dispose of. Plastics have a low melting point, ranging anywhere from 190–400 degrees.

From there, it can be turned into anything or just simply disposed of. I'll let my team search for the murder weapon. In the meantime, I'll focus my attention on bringing in suspects. Elements of this case remind me of the cold case I had solved years ago.

The most promising piece of evidence is a DNA sample collected from a minor scratch on Sullivan's left cheek. No matches to the DNA have been found in our criminal database.

The coroner says this injury could have been caused by anyone accidentally grazing his face with their fingernail and didn't necessarily occur during his murder. I, on the other hand, think a fresh cut on his face may lead us to a suspect.

Taking out my notebook, I plan out my next steps in the investigation. Before tracking down Davis or Natalia, I need to pay a visit to the crime scene. After the scene has been processed, I go in to sweep the area for anything that may have been overlooked.

Sometimes, my team focuses on the smaller details to such a degree that they miss something obvious, something hidden in plain sight.

My concentration is disrupted by a heavy-handed pound on the door. *I know that knock. It's the Deputy Chief. Here we go.*

"Come in," I beckon in a smooth, unbothered tone.

The door swings open. Deputy Chief Forbes stands in the doorway but doesn't look intent on staying long.

Always so heavy-handed, so forceful. What are you trying to prove? I smile and fold my hands on my desk, waiting for him to speak first.

"What's this 'bout taking a trip alone to visit the victim's parents, Ms. Taylor? Who authorized your travel?"

I clear my throat and sit up a little straighter. "It's Commander Taylor, *Deputy* Chief," I emphasize *Deputy* to remind him that he too has to answer to someone above him.

"I bet I can guess who told you. The same person you believe should be sitting in this chair instead of me." My eyes bore into his, forcing him to look away.

"In the future, you're to request authorization and backup, er—"

"Commander. Why is it so difficult for you to address me accordingly?"

Forbes shifts his weight uncomfortably. "I'ma let you off with a warning. Your position doesn't give you full sovereignty. I wanna update on this case, on my desk, by the end of the day today." With that, he turns and leaves as abruptly as he came.

I'm not provoked by him at all. Whether he wants to come to terms with it or not, he's on his way out. I can almost smell his powerlessness when he's in my presence. His dismissive attitude toward me is his weak attempt to conceal his cowardice.

I've overheard whispers in our department about his incompetence and our superiors working to force him into retirement. Solving this case should make my promotion to Deputy Chief a shoo-in.

At least, if I were a man, solving this case would make my promotion to Deputy Chief a shoo-in. I'm going to have to do something spectacular to secure this promotion. Something akin to landing my promotion to Commander.

New Year's Eve, 2015 (31 Years Old)

West Englewood, Chicago

I look over at Ezra in the passenger seat of our unmarked patrol car. *He always lets me in the driver's seat and I know that has to bother him at times.* I smile to myself.

"What are you smiling about?" Ezra asks playfully.

"Oh, just wondering, if we're going to make it to the pub in time to see the ball drop."

"If this guy hurries up and commits the crime, then yeah, we'll make it," he replies with uncertainty as he pulls the binoculars to his face for the umpteenth time.

We've been staking out the house for six hours. This is the part of my job that I absolutely loathe, the waiting. Waiting for the drug addicts to arrive. Waiting for illegal substances to change hands.

After the third or fourth hour, there's always suspicion that our cover has been somehow blown. There's always the possibility that we're wasting our time.

As the minutes slowly pass, my smile fades. I feel a wave of aggravation and restlessness. My body noticeably tenses up. So noticeably that Ezra reaches over and gently touches my hand. I pull my hand away and our eyes meet.

"Mila," Ezra starts.

"No, Ezra. I know you're just trying to help me relax, but we agreed. We agreed to keep our boundaries. We're partners. That's it."

"I know you don't really believe that."

"Believe what?"

"That we're only partners. Especially after—"

"Ezra, stop. Focus. This," I point back and forth between us, "has to stay professional. It's already interfering with our job."

"How, Mila? How is it interfering? Look around. Nothing's happening right now." He motions at the house where there are still no signs of life.

"Exactly. Nothing's happening," I direct this statement at him and he understands the true meaning behind it.

There's a piercing silence. I take note of the time, thirty minutes until the ball drop.

"I'm ready to throw in the towel for the night. Someone must've tipped him off." I reach for the radio.

"I applied for a transfer to the Detective's Bureau," Ezra interpolates.

I pull my hand back from the radio. "Oh? I didn't know you were interested." I feel slightly jaded. All the time we spend together while on the job and it's the first I'm hearing of this.

Ezra shifts his body so he's able to look at me straight-on without having to turn his head. "You've never asked. As a matter of fact, with all the time we spend together, you never ask me much about anything, Mila." Ezra is now giving off wounded animal vibes.

"Well, I'm asking now. What division?" I'm not sure if I'm asking more out of concern or curiosity.

"Forensic Services."

My eyebrows rise. "Does this have something to do with—?"

"Oh, so you do listen."

"Seriously, Ezra? Now, you're just being childish. I could never forget about Benny. Of course, I didn't know him like you did, but Benny's cold case has kept me up at night."

"Has it really?"

"Yes, the details of your brother's murder have plagued me. I can only imagine how it's affected you. At least with my sister—"

"You had closure," Ezra interjected.

"Yes, I had closure." I lower my head, feeling remorse for how careless I've been with Ezra's emotions when he's clearly battling his own demons.

Ezra and Benny weren't just fraternal twins. They were partners. Back then, I was only an acquaintance. I remember admiring their light-hearted and lively banter when I responded to a few calls with them. It was apparent that they were joined at the hip.

Both cut from the same cloth, stand-up and reliable guys. That's why when asked to take Benny's place as Ezra's partner, I knew I would never be able to fill Benny's shoes but would at least have the confidence that my partner had my back.

On the night of Benny's murder in 2013, Ezra dropped him off at his apartment building after working a shift. Benny never made it into his building. Security footage shows Ezra's patrol car pulling away as Benny approaches the entrance.

It then captures Benny pausing and looking in the direction of the alley running between his building and the building next door. He oddly walks into the alley and disappears from the camera's view.

That's where his body was found the next day. I was off that day but Ezra was the first at the scene. The scene appeared to be a robbery. Benny's wallet was missing, but his cell phone and badge were still on his person.

Cause of death, strangulation. Ezra watched hours upon hours of security footage and never caught sight of a person going into or out of the alley. It was evident that the perpetrator entered and exited another way, but how?

This is the question that plagues Ezra's mind to this day. When a case of someone you don't know goes cold, it's tough enough on the psyche. Imagine the impact of never knowing who your brother's killer is. Knowing that evil still lurks in the streets and you may never see justice.

Ezra's right. I rarely ask him questions, especially about Benny. There was one time I asked him why they never got an apartment together. Two bachelors, ruling the world. Ezra said since they worked together and spent a lot of their free time together, they needed something to separate them.

A way to maintain their individual identities and personal space. If you're around anyone for too long, blood or not, it's bound to eventually ruin your relationship. He knew he didn't know everything about his brother and his brother didn't know everything about him.

You don't have to know everything to be close to someone. His response made sense to me but I know the 'what ifs' still plague him. What if they had been roommates? Would Benny still be alive today?

On this night, New Year's Eve, Ezra's pain suddenly feels magnetic. Maybe it's the fact that it's almost midnight. Maybe it's knowing that I'm the source of some of his pain.

Before I can stop myself, I grab him by the lapel and pull him against me, kissing him deeply. He briefly forgets that he's upset with me and gives in before pulling away.

"Stop." He breaks away, breathing heavily. "Stop. I don't need your pity."

Facing forward in the driver's seat, I respond coldly, "Just so you know, I applied for a transfer, too." I start the car and pull away from the curb.

Within two months of our conversation in the patrol car, Ezra and I transferred to the Detective's Bureau. Within the year, I was promoted to the Commander's position of the Forensic Services division for solving Benny's cold case.

On the night of Benny's murder in 2013, Ezra dropped him off at his apartment building after working a shift. Benny never made it into his building. Security footage shows Ezra's patrol car pulling away as Benny approaches the entrance.

It then captures Benny pausing and looking in the direction of the alley running between his building and the building next door. He oddly walks into the alley and disappears from the camera's view.

That's where his body was found the next day. I was off that day but Ezra was the first at the scene. The scene appeared to be a robbery. Benny's wallet was missing, but his cell phone and badge were still on his person.

Cause of death, strangulation. Ezra watched hours upon hours of security footage and never caught sight of a person going into or out of the alley. It was evident that the perpetrator entered and exited another way, but how?

This is the question that plagues Ezra's mind to this day. When a case of someone you don't know goes cold, it's tough enough on the psyche. Imagine the impact of never knowing who your brother's killer is. Knowing that evil still lurks in the streets and you may never see justice.

Ezra's right. I rarely ask him questions, especially about Benny. There was one time I asked him why they never got an apartment together. Two bachelors, ruling the world. Ezra said since they worked together and spent a lot of their free time together, they needed something to separate them.

A way to maintain their individual identities and personal space. If you're around anyone for too long, blood or not, it's bound to eventually ruin your relationship. He knew he didn't know everything about his brother and his brother didn't know everything about him.

You don't have to know everything to be close to someone. His response made sense to me but I know the 'what ifs' still plague him. What if they had been roommates? Would Benny still be alive today?

On this night, New Year's Eve, Ezra's pain suddenly feels magnetic. Maybe it's the fact that it's almost midnight. Maybe it's knowing that I'm the source of some of his pain.

Before I can stop myself, I grab him by the lapel and pull him against me, kissing him deeply. He briefly forgets that he's upset with me and gives in before pulling away.

"Stop." He breaks away, breathing heavily. "Stop. I don't need your pity."

Facing forward in the driver's seat, I respond coldly, "Just so you know, I applied for a transfer, too." I start the car and pull away from the curb.

Within two months of our conversation in the patrol car, Ezra and I transferred to the Detective's Bureau. Within the year, I was promoted to the Commander's position of the Forensic Services division for solving Benny's cold case.

Present Day
9 October 2024

Sullivan Maxwell's Apartment W. Madison St.

I'm standing at the center of Sullivan's 505 sq. ft. studio apartment. After a brief interview with the doorman, Joe Krider, he let me into the apartment. Joe didn't have any additional information to offer.

The security camera footage has already been reviewed by my team and turned in as evidence. The footage shows Sullivan leaving his apartment for work in the morning and returning unaccompanied to his apartment after work that evening.

The next person to enter Sully's apartment was Joe the following morning. He was completing a wellness check after Sully didn't leave for work at the usual time.

When you enter the front door of Sully's apartment, there's a hallway leading to the only bathroom on the left, a closet on the right and the rest of the apartment lay straight ahead.

The hallway walls are bare, most likely because it's too narrow to decorate. The living room, which doubles as a bedroom with a pull-out couch, reveals Sully's character. Bookshelves filled with books of all genres line most of the wall space.

Framed family portraits are sprinkled throughout. I recognize some of these portraits from the walls of Sullivan's parents' house. Sully's quilt is neatly folded on the couch with his pillow carefully laid on top.

He never made it to bed that night. There's a worn forest green armchair in the corner of the room. A floor lamp attached to an end table covered in books and newspapers indicates this is where he spent most of his leisure.

A laptop lay on the red oak coffee table in front of it. I'm not surprised the laptop wasn't bagged as evidence. This is what I mean by Ezra overlooking the larger details. With gloved hands, I slide the laptop into the large plastic evidence bag. I lay it back down on the coffee table to resume my search.

From the case file, there was a coffee mug next to the laptop. The mug was bagged as evidence to collect a DNA sample. It was the same mug that the fingerprint was lifted from. In the crime scene photos, it was half full.

I picture Sully sipping on a cup of coffee as he scrolled through his laptop. His fate unbeknownst to him. There were no signs of struggle, which indicates Sully's visitor was someone he knew.

Without opening the balcony door, I peer out to see a lonely potted plant and one singular lawn chair. Since we're on the third floor, there's a fire escape. The team already swept the balcony for prints, so I pivot to take a closer look at the portraits neatly placed in between the breaks in the lines of books on the shelves.

One in particular catches my eye, a twenty-something Sullivan standing in comradery with another young adult male. They're posing for a photo in front of what is now *Sully's Read n Sip*. Except the marquee in this photo says *M&P's Read n Sip. Maxwell and Parks.*

This must've been taken during the grand opening of Sullivan and Davis' shop. It's a shame their brotherhood was destroyed by business. I slip the photo into a small evidence bag. I may need this to help me track down Davis Parks.

I lay the second piece of bagged evidence on top of the laptop. Then stare at the dark kitchen, the spot where the crime was committed. Joe had found Sully's body on the kitchen floor.

Connected to the living room, the kitchen only allows for a few major appliances and just enough space for one person to move around comfortably. Sully had been backed into a small space with no escape. I move to flick on the kitchen light.

"Natalia?" I hear a voice behind me and whirl around.

A slight, elderly gentleman wearing an oversized brown sweater, khakis, and loafers stands before me. He's squinting with a grim expression on his face.

Taken aback, I flash my badge as I say, "No, sir. I'm Commander Mila Taylor from the Chicago Detective's Bureau."

The gentleman puts his hand to his forehead. "Oh, forgive me, Commander. I've misplaced my glasses. You just look similar to—well, never mind then. Without my glasses, I'm blind as a bat." He squints slightly harder.

"Who are you?" I ask as I take a step backward.

"How rude of me. I'm Frank Brewer. I live in the apartment across from here. Sullivan and I were friends. Please excuse my intrusion. I just saw the door open and—"

"Do you normally walk into a person's house when the door is left open, Mr. Brewer?" I ask suspiciously.

"Oh no, Commander. I would never." Now, Frank is the one taking a step back as he waves his hands in the air and shakes his head.

"What can you tell me about Natalia?" I can tell I've caught him off guard. I went from being accusatory to asking investigative questions.

"Um, well. I don't know much about her. Sully was a very private person. The only reason I know anything at all is because I stopped by a few months ago to ask for help with my internet."

"My blasted internet signal is always going out. Sully always dropped everything to help me. He was such a good man." Frank's eyes fill with tears. He takes out a neatly folded handkerchief to blow his nose before continuing. I wait patiently for him to resume.

"Where was I? Oh right, I stopped by a few months ago, the night of June 8, to be exact. That's when I saw a glimpse of a fair lady seated in his living room. I wasn't wearing my glasses but I was able to make out a few details."

"She had dark hair, darker than yours, now that I think of it. Fair complexion. I thought it odd that she was wearing all black clothing. Unfortunately, I wasn't able to get a closer look because Sully ushered me back over to my place without an introduction."

"On his way out, I heard him say, 'I'll be right back, Natalia'. He fixed my internet that night but very little was said about his company. I didn't want to pry but managed to ask if his guest would be staying long. He reluctantly said, 'No, she's leaving tonight'."

"This whole encounter didn't seem extremely odd to you?" I've taken out my notebook and am scribbling a few notes.

"It did. That's why the next morning, I went straight to Joe, our doorman, and asked if a guest by the name of Natalia had signed in. There was no record of anyone named Natalia visiting the night before or ever."

"As a matter of fact, Joe said no one accompanied Sully into or out of the building that night either." Frank shivers and wraps his arms around his body. "I'm beginning to think I imagined the whole thing. I am on new meds for anxiety. The doc warned me about the possibility of hallucinations."

"Why didn't you share this information with Detective Wilkins or any of the other officers on the scene?"

"I was out of town visiting my son in Wisconsin. I got back yesterday morning and have been devastated since hearing the news. When I saw Sully's door open, part of me hoped to come in here and find him sitting in his chair reading a book." Frank gazes longingly at Sully's green armchair as if he's picturing him sitting there right now.

I look at my watch. It's nearly 3. My stomach grumbles and I remember that I haven't eaten at all today.

"Thank you for your time, Mr. Brewer. I'm going to have to ask you to leave now. This is the scene of a crime. I wouldn't want your fingerprints getting mixed up in the investigation."

"Right. No, I wouldn't want that either. I'll head back to my apartment now."

"Please take my card in case you think of anything else." I pass the card to him.

He looks down at it. Then, looks at me solemnly as he nods in agreement before turning and leaving the way he came.

10 November 2016
(32 Years Old)

Bureau of Detectives, Forensic Services Division, Commander Forbes' Office

"I have a lead on the Wilkins case, Sir. Permission to follow-up with it," I address Commander Forbes.

"Benny Wilkins," Commander Forbes eyes me apprehensively.

"Yessir." I await Forbes' response. He doesn't respond which tells me he wants more details. "My informant says a guy named Deek is selling fake IDs."

"Yeah, so?" Forbes rests his husky elbows on his desk. The intertwined hairs on his arms remind me of a bird's nest.

"So, Deek tried to sell him an ID of a guy named Bennett Wilkins. Benny's wallet went missing on the night of his murder." I struggle to cover up the annoyance I feel from having to explain this.

Forbes' dark eyes widen. "Take Ezra with you and I want a full report by the end of the day."

"But Sir, Ezra was too close to the victim. That would be a conflict of interests, wouldn't you agree?" Forbes and

I briefly make eye contact until he flinches and looks away. He never could look me in the eye longer than a few seconds.

I watch him run his hands through his receding salt and pepper hair. "Yeah, ok. Don't take Ezra, but if you need backup—"

"I'll call if I need backup. Thank you, Sir." I hurry out before he can change his mind.

I've heard rumors that our Deputy Chief is preparing to announce his retirement, which means Forbes is likely to take his place. At least, he's banking on that outcome. Rumor also has it that Forbes has his prospects on Ezra taking his place as Commander.

Ever since day one at the bureau, Forbes has treated Ezra like a son. Too bad for him, Chief Cromwell makes the final decision.

I take a left on W. 79th and pull into a side street. I'm in an unmarked car but won't take any chances. I reach in the back seat and grab the handle to my duffle bag. Unzipping it, I take inventory of my navy-blue hoodie, gray sweatpants, brunette wig, and sneakers.

While dumping the contents of the bag onto the passenger seat, I fish around for a hair tie and use it to toss my hair up into a messy bun. After pulling the hoodie on, the oversized sweatpants slip over my dress pants.

I lace and tie my sneakers. Then, secure and straighten the wig. While checking my reflection in the rearview, I consider going for a short brown bob the next time I visit the salon. It brings out the brown in my eyes.

The sidewalk leading to the suspect's apartment building is uneven. Overgrown hedges line the perimeter.

The green paint on the siding is cracked and peeling. There's no intercom system and the main door is ajar.

As soon as I enter, the scent of stale cigarettes and urine hits me. *Classy place. I can't believe Benny lived in the building right next door.*

I walk up two flights of stairs and knock on apartment 312. The tenant keeps the chain on the door but glares at me through the narrow opening.

"What do you want?" Deek demands gruffly.

"I was told you could help me." I flash a wad of cash from my sweatpants pocket.

His eyes remain where the cash once was. "Who sent you?"

"Rick."

"Hmph. Hold on." The door closes and I hear him unfastening the chain. Within seconds, the door opens and he motions me in.

As soon as I'm a few feet into the apartment, he closes and deadbolts the door. I turn to face him, ready to overpower him if needed. Standing at 5'8, my height has always been a deterrent to men considering any funny business.

"Relax, sweetheart. I'm not gon' try nothin'." Deek holds up his hands and pauses to look me up and down. "What you need a fake ID for? You don't look younger n' twenty-one."

"That's my business. Are you good for it?" I watch him walk over to a desk and pull out the top drawer.

"Lemme see if I have somethin' for you." As he rifles through the drawer, I spot what I came here for. A tan leather wallet, similar to Benny's, is tucked in the corner.

His bony hand holds up an ID of a middle-aged woman, curly brown hair, and green eyes. "What 'bout this one?"

I shake my head. "My hair's straight and my eyes are hazel."

"You're a tough one, huh?" He resumes his search.

"Alright. How 'bout this one?" He holds up another middle-aged woman, straight, light brown hair, and hazel eyes.

"Nah, the hair's too light." I shake my head.

"Alright, lady. I don't have nothin' for you then." He slams the drawer aggressively.

"Can't you get me something better?" I pat the pocket with the cash.

"I need a few days but I'll get you what you're asking for. It's gonna be double though."

"That's fine. I'll come back in a few days. I also need something for a male friend."

"Was he look like?"

"5'5, dark brown hair, blue eyes, olive skin—"

Before I can finish, Deek flings the drawer open and grabs the wallet. He opens it and holds it up to me. It's empty with the exception of an Illinois State License registered to Bennett Wilkins All the credit cards and any money or photos Benny may have kept in it are missing.

"Oh, that's perfect. Can you hold it for him?"

"Why can't you get it for him now?"

"I want him to see it first."

"Look, lady. I don't know you from Adam." Deek steps closer to me. "I oughta just take that money outta your pocket—"

Before he can consider his next move, I have a gun pointed at his head.

He backs up with his hands raised. "Alright, a woman protectin' herself. I can respect that. I don't want no problems. Come back in a few days and I'll have what you're lookin' for."

I gesture toward the door, signaling him to unlock it. He quickly obeys my order. Once my feet hit the pavement, I tuck the gun away and take off running. I don't want him following me.

Two days later, I'm back at Deek's apartment but this time, I have a search warrant and a few officers for backup. Deek's arrested under prima facie. In plain English, it means at first view.

In law terms, it means the evidence was legally sufficient to establish a case against him. Deek predictably pleads not guilty, claiming he was framed and he has never seen Benny in his life.

However, Deek's rap sheet of dealing, theft, and fraud made it difficult for him to prove his innocence. Between Benny's stolen wallet and ID in his possession and no one to corroborate his alibi for the night of Benny's murder, the jury found him guilty.

Deek was sentenced to 30 years in prison.

Present Day
9 October 2024

Aurora, Illinois

Of course, Sully's laptop is password encrypted. After processing it as evidence, I drop it off with my best IT guy. While he's working on cracking the password, I prepare to pay a visit to Davis Parks.

His address was easy to locate but his residence is about an hour outside of Chicago in a suburb in Aurora. Davis has a clean record and is married with two kids, ages 4 and 6. It turns out Tabitha never got a job after college.

She's a homemaker and there's nothing wrong with that. It just makes it look like she forced Davis to abandon Sullivan so she could stay at home. She wanted Davis to get a corporate job, so his salary alone could support their lifestyle.

If I leave now, I'll arrive at his place around supper time and should be able to catch him at home.

Davis' neighborhood is picture perfect with fresh cut lawns, new asphalt roads, brick two-story homes, and children playing tag in their yards while parents sit on the porch and chat. That's how I find Davis and his wife, Tabitha; chit chatting with a neighbor as they watch their children play outside. I park on the curb across the street so as not to startle the children.

Davis's expression distinctly changes as he sees me approach. He's mid-laugh when I catch his eye. Straight-faced, he says something inaudible to his wife and neighbor. Before I'm halfway up the driveway, he beckons his children to come inside.

"Julianna, Charlie, time to come in and wash up for supper." Davis opens the front door and beckons his children into the house.

His wife follows behind and quickly shuts the door. The neighbor ushers past me with her child, barely giving me eye contact. It's almost as if they knew I was coming or they know why I'm here.

"I know who you are and I know why you're here," Davis says as he walks down the porch steps and meets me on the sidewalk.

I stop a few feet in front of him. "You know who I am?"

"Well, not who you are but I know who you represent. You're law enforcement."

"Why do you assume that?"

"Look, Miss—"

"Detective Taylor." I flash my badge methodically.

"Detective Taylor, I know about my old friend's early demise. I was notified by his employee immediately. I knew it was only a matter of time before someone would show up here."

"I would've preferred to be called into the precinct though. Coming to my home, with my wife and kids—is this really necessary?"

"It depends on what you tell me about the last time you saw your old friend."

"Hold on. I was his college friend turned business partner. Since when does that make me a suspect?" Davis is clearly becoming contentious.

"No one said you're a suspect, Mr. Parks. Just answer a few questions and then I'll be on my way. If I need to speak to you again, I'll set up an interview at the precinct. How does that sound?"

Davis looks up at the sky as if he's considering the offer. After a few moments, he concedes, "Alright. But this is as close as we're getting to my home. I don't want my kids overhearing our conversation."

"Understood. Do I have permission to record?"

Davis grunts and nods begrudgingly. I set my bag down on the sidewalk and stoop to retrieve my recorder. Since I'm forced to stand here awkwardly in the middle of the sidewalk, I'll just listen to the recording later and take notes then.

After pressing record, the questions commence.

"Mr. Parks, what was the nature of your relationship with Sullivan Maxwell?"

"Sullivan and I met in college, Northern Illinois University. We had common interests and quickly became best friends. After graduation, we moved to Chicago together and opened a second-hand bookstore and cafe."

"That was in 2014. By 2017, things weren't going well. Business hadn't picked up the way we'd hoped. I was dating

Tabby and we were getting pretty serious, talking about marriage and children. She was finishing up her teaching degree at the University of Chicago but didn't want to teach or raise a family in Chicago."

"Her family is here in Aurora. I had to think about her and our future, so I approached Sully about selling the business or, at least, allowing me to sell my portion of the business. He didn't handle the news well."

"What do you mean by that?"

"He wrote me off—literally. I asked him to be the best man at our wedding and he never responded. He didn't even attend as a guest. He met my children for the first time two years ago."

"The only reason why he met them is his parents were renewing their vows and invited us to attend. We were really close before all this happened. His parents still kept in touch even when he didn't." Davis' eyes begin to water and he takes a deep breath.

"Why do you think Sully reacted so harshly?"

Davis looks at me with a befuddled expression. "Really? I was his business partner and I abandoned him. I don't blame him at all for his reaction. If the tables were turned, I may have done the same."

"Yeah, but, he had to understand that your vision changed. It often does as you get older. When you were talking about getting married to Tabitha, you weren't the same Davis who was roommates in college with Sullivan."

"I appreciate your empathy. I did what I had to do. I just wish it hadn't been at the cost of losing my best friend and now—"

"He's gone," I finish his sentence so he doesn't have to.

Tears stream down his cheeks and Davis turns away from me to preserve his pride.

"The last time you saw and spoke to Sully was at the renewal of his parents' vows two years ago. What was that interaction like?"

Davis uses his sleeves to wipe his face. "It was cordial. We had a couple beers together and reminisced about the old days. I thought we had connected again and he had finally forgiven me. But then, a few weeks later, when I tried to call him, he didn't answer and never returned my phone call."

"And how did you find out about his death?"

"One of Sully's employees, James, called me as soon as he found out."

"How did James know to call you?"

"Oh, James has worked for the shop since the grand opening. He's Sully's oldest and most loyal employee."

"Gotcha. Thank you for your time, Mr. Parks. I don't have any further questions at this time." I stop recording and pull out my card. As I extend it to him, he's reluctant to take it.

"Mr. Parks, if you don't want to be considered a suspect. Then, I strongly suggest you cooperate."

"Is that a threat?"

"No, it's sound advice. Take it or leave it."

With that, Davis takes the card and shoves it into his pocket without looking at it.

"Am I free to go into my house and rejoin my family?" He asks sarcastically.

"Yessir, enjoy your evening." I give a casual wave of the hand, grab my bag from the pavement, and return to my car.

On the drive back to Chicago, one part of our conversation replays in my mind. Davis said he approached Sully about selling his portion of the company but never confirms that he actually did it.

New Year's Eve, 2016
(32 Years Old)

Downtown Chicago

I hear faint noises outside my office door and look up to see Ezra staring in.

"I'm heading over to the pub to watch the ball drop. Wanted to see if you wanna go for old time's sake," he asks sheepishly.

I look at my watch. *How is it already 10:30?*

"You know what? Yeah, that'd be nice." I stand and stretch. I've been pouring over the same case file for over three hours. My eyes are dry and sticky and my head slightly aches from the tension. My neck and shoulders are stiff from sitting in the same position for too long.

"I'll meet you at the car then?" Ezra asks optimistically.

"Your car or mine?" I counter.

"You still prefer to drive, right?" He really intends it as a rhetorical question but I nod anyway. "Let's take yours then."

I can't help but smile as he practically skips out of my office. I flip the case file closed and gather my coat and handbag to head to the car.

Ezra and I haven't been alone like this since the stakeout last New Year's Eve. The first few minutes of the drive are silent.

"What's new with you besides the normal office stuff?" I break through the silence.

"I'm taking some personal leave the second week of January to go see my parents for a week. I haven't been home since Benny's—" He doesn't need to finish. I already know.

"That's great! I'm glad to hear that you're taking some time off for yourself. I know your parents are excited to see you," I rave cheerfully.

"They don't know yet. I'm gonna let it be a surprise."

"Ok, even better!" I gush.

"Yeah, I suppose." Ezra's voice is suddenly monotone. It's unusual that he wouldn't be looking forward to visiting his parents.

In an effort to lighten the mood, I say, "Well, please tell them I say 'hello'."

"Right," Ezra scoffs.

I'm taken aback by this sudden change in attitude. We drive the rest of the way in silence.

The pub is warm and smells of beer and cigars. This is one of few places left that you can still smoke indoors. Ezra and I are lucky to find two vacant seats at the bar. It's noisier than usual tonight.

I take note that there are mostly men here, all in good spirits. That's a relief. I would hate to ruin my New Year's by breaking up a bar brawl.

Ezra and I order beers on tap. I'm not sipping. I'm gulping my first mug. The ice-cold beverage slides down my throat.

"Geez, rough week?" Ezra snorts as he pokes fun at me.

I wipe my mouth with a napkin and laugh.

"You should come with me to see my parents," Ezra states nonchalantly.

I nearly choke on my drink. "What?"

"Yeah, you haven't seen them in a while. They've been asking about you."

"Ezra, that would be unprofessional. I'm the Commander now."

"Yeah, so?"

"I'm your—"

"Superior. Boss. I still don't see what the big deal is."

"Are you trying to get me removed from my position? Going on a personal trip with you just wouldn't look good."

The warmth of the pub, the alcohol, and the heated conversation is making me sweat. I remove my blazer and loosen my sleeveless blouse from my pants. I look over at Ezra just in time to catch him watching me. He turns away as soon as I notice.

The words he mumbles as he looks away leave me dumbfounded, "What doesn't look good is how you moved into your position."

The bartender notices my empty glass and asks if I need a refill. I nod, thank him, and force a smile.

Then, turning back to Ezra, I ask, "What's that supposed to mean?"

"We all want to know how you did it, Mila."

"Did what?"

His blue eyes blaze with suspicion. "How you caught Benny's killer on your own."

"Who's *all*? And what do you mean on my own? I got a warrant, and I had backup."

"*All* is everyone in the bureau, except the one who promoted you. How did you know to get a warrant?"

"I've told you this story. I went undercover."

"How did you know to go undercover?"

"I had an informant."

"Who?" Ezra hasn't broken eye contact. It reminds me that he's the only person I know who can look me in the eyes for longer than a few seconds.

"You know I can't tell you that. I have to protect the people who tip me off."

"Right. And you were trying to protect me by not including me in any of it? Don't you think I would want to be the one to catch my brother's murderer?"

"That's what this is about? You're upset because we didn't let you do the arrest? You might've killed Deek. You know we couldn't let you get near him. You wouldn't have been able to control your emotions."

"Who's we? It's you. YOU didn't let me do the arrest. You have no idea what I might've done. You really don't know me at all, Mila. You were selfish and you know it. It wasn't about Benny at all. You had your mind set on the Commander position and you used Benny to get it."

"Wow. I really thought solving his case would bring you closure. Now, I see it just made you jealous and spiteful."

"Closure? Hah. We don't even know if Deek killed him. Prima facie is not closure, honey. It's just bad luck for Deek, who by unfortunate circumstance, may be serving time for a crime he didn't even do."

Ezra orders a shot from the bartender and knocks it back.

I say in a low voice, "It's unfortunate you feel that way."

Suddenly, there's a jovial uproar between two guys in their twenties sitting on the other side of me. Ezra and I both look at them.

The two men have their arms stretched across each other's shoulders and neck and are swaying back and forth. It's evident they've had their fair amount of spirits. Still, something about their laughter and light-heartedness draws me to them.

I lean over and hold my glass up to the young men. They lift their glasses to mine. "Cheers!" We say in unison.

I let out a full belly laugh and look over at Ezra. His stool is empty. I scan the room in time to see him exiting the pub. He doesn't look back.

Let him leave then.

"Is that your boyfriend leaving without you?" The young man with the chestnut brown hair and light brown eyes asks earnestly.

"Oh no, we're just colleagues." My eyes are still on the door, wondering if he'll change his mind and come back in.

"That's some colleague to leave you alone on New Year's Eve," the other young man with sandy hair and grayish eyes chimes in.

I turn back to the gentlemen. "He's just going through some things, you know."

"We get it. We're here celebrating a new year as our dreams are slowly dying," the chestnut-haired man replies matter-of-factly yet with a goofy smile on his face.

"I'm sorry to hear that," I respond sympathetically.

The other man adds, "I'm sorry my friend is being a downer. We started a business, straight out of college, and we were both hoping it would take off by now. But cheers to the possibilities in a new year!" He holds up his glass and we all cheers and drink together.

A young blonde woman with bouncy chin-length hair and blue eyes rushes over and pops her head between me and the man with sandy hair. She says, "Happy New Year, sweetheart!" and kisses him on the cheek. Her bubbly, singsong tone is nauseating.

Their lips lock as his friend and I look away awkwardly. After a few minutes of making out, the guy breaks away and gestures in my direction while saying, "Unless this nice lady offers to move down one, we havta move so we have room for my sweetie."

Gross. "Uh, yeah, of course," I reply.

Understanding what he's asking, I grab my belongings and scooch over to the empty seat. *Ezra's not coming back.*

The young woman and I exchange half smiles as she slides onto the seat next to me and her beau. I glance at the other guy who has quickly become the third wheel. He appears perturbed as he stares intently at the TV. Looks like we both lost our companions tonight.

I sip my beer and watch the TV as I listen to the conversation between the blonde woman and her boyfriend. I'm really not intending to eavesdrop but we're sitting so closely, I can't avoid overhearing.

"Have you told him yet?" She tries to whisper but it's so loud in here, it's more of a deep, low voice.

"Hush. No, it's not the right time. Please be patient." He looks over at his friend who's still sipping his beer and watching TV.

"You know I graduate in May. We've talked about this. I want to move back home as soon as I'm handed my degree. We need to start preparing now."

"I know. Just give me a few more weeks."

She lets out a sound of disgust. She's clearly tired of waiting for him to tell his friend whatever it is. It surprises me that she doesn't just tell him herself. Out of the corner of my eye, I see him wrap his arm around her and pull her close. He whispers something in her ear and she giggles.

Men are so manipulative.

Eventually, my thoughts drown out the noise around me, including their conversation. After the ball drops, I pay my tab and give a friendly wave to the three strangers who in an odd way kept me company tonight.

I'm halfway to the exit when the guy with the chestnut hair calls, "If you're ever on W. Madison, come see us at M&P—!" The noisy bar drowns out the rest of his sentence. I turn and give him a thumbs up with no real intentions of following through.

In the early morning hours, I sit on the floor in my bedroom and pull a large shoe box out from under my bed. I rest the box in my lap and run my hand across the top, watching clumps of dust float into the air and land on the carpet around me. I set aside the top and observe the contents. Several sealed letters addressed to me from a patient at the Chester Mental Institution lay delicately at the bottom of the box. That patient is my dad. My hands tremble as I open the letters for the first time.

With each letter, my resentment intensifies but not because we're so different. As I read, it's apparent that we have more in common that I'd like to admit.

Present Day
10 October 2024

Bureau of Detectives, Forensic Services Division

My cell phone rings at 7:30 am.

"Please tell me you have good news, Levi." I hold my breath in anticipation.

"I cracked the password, boss," Levi boasts proudly.

"And that's why I call you my best IT guy," I butter him up. "When can I pick it up from you?"

"I'll be in the office around 9."

"9 it is. Thanks, Levi. I knew I could count on you." I hang up the phone and take a bite of my croissant. I wash it down with a sip of black coffee.

I didn't sleep last night, yet another sleepless night. Instead of tossing and turning, I got dressed and walked to a nearby diner. That's where I am now.

I arrive at Levi's office a little before 9. He hasn't arrived yet, so I sit down and scroll through my phone. I have a missed call from Ezra.

"Good morning, Commander!" I hear a cheery voice and look up to see Levi entering the office with the laptop under his arm.

He sets it down on the desk and removes his hat and coat. As he hangs his coat on a hook, he says, "I know you're gonna need me to do more than unlock the laptop. Ezra has me doing all kinds of things with Sullivan's cell phone."

"Wait, what? You have Sullivan's phone?"

"Eh, yah. I thought you knew."

"No, that piece of evidence wasn't shared with me. What kind of things is Ezra having you do?"

"Well, I'm trying to get into the darn thing first. Believe it or not, it's easier to crack a laptop password than a cell phone. Wouldn't it be nice if he used the same password for both? Once I'm in, I've been instructed to create a log of his phone calls, text messages, photos, you know the routine."

"Yeah, I know. Notify me when that log is ready."

"Will do. Now, let's get to this laptop." Levi puts on a pair of latex gloves and hands a pair to me. Then he sits behind his desk and flips it open. "I removed the password protection, so you don't have to log in at all now."

"May I?" I ask as I slide the laptop toward me with gloved hands.

Levi jumps up and offers me his seat. I accept. Sullivan's desktop is well-organized with several neatly aligned labeled folders. *Where to start?*

Almost as if he's reading my mind, Levi suggests, "Why don't you look at his emails?"

I click on the email application and let out a sigh of relief when it opens without needing a password. His inbox has 1,232 emails.

Levi takes one look and says, "This is gonna take a while. Why don't I go get us some coffee?"

I nod and smile. He leaves the office and I begin reading, starting with the most recent email. When he returns, I'm only on the tenth email. I say thanks as he hands me a cup of coffee.

"I'm not tryna overstep, boss, but if you're lookin' for correspondence, ya might wanna start with his sent mail."

"Good call." I take a sip of the steamy black coffee and click on sent.

At first, most of Sully's correspondence is related to his business. Messages between him and vendors. There are invoices here and there for repairs and inspections done at the shop.

One of the invoices catches my attention. The date of the repair was 17 July 2024 and it's billed to Sullivan Maxwell and Davis Parks.

Why would Davis' name be on an invoice from this year? I keep these thoughts to myself but make a mental note to uncover more information.

I nudge Levi and point to the screen. "Look. There's an email from June 25th of this year to someone with the screenname sweet4you. Sully says, *Please don't leave. I can make it worthwhile for you to stay. I promise you won't regret it. I love you.*"

I click below his reply to see the rest of the thread. "It appears sweet4you wrote to Sully first. She says, *Dear Sullivan, I've been offered an opportunity to teach abroad and I accepted it. By the time you read this, I'll be on a flight. You're a very special man and you're going to make a woman very happy someday. Love, Natalia.* Well, there's that. She broke his heart and left the country."

"You've heard of this woman named Natalia?" Levi asks with raised eyebrows.

"Sully's parents and his neighbor mentioned something about her."

"We should trace her IP address to see if she really left the country," Levi advises.

"I agree but first, I need to finish going through these emails. You need to work on the phone's passcode, so I'll get out of your way. I'll be in my office if you need me." Levi nods in agreement. With my coffee in one hand and Sullivan's laptop in the other, I head to my office.

I really just want to investigate the unusual billing on my own. Back in my office, I scan the desktop folders and click on the folder entitled 'Tax Documents'.

Within this folder, there are multiple folders dated by year. I open '2023'. Sure enough, Davis' name is on all the tax documents related to *Sully's Read n Sip*.

He didn't sell his share after all.

I realize none of this makes sense. Why all the drama and the strained friendship if Davis never sold his share of the business? It's time to call Davis Parks and schedule that second interview at the precinct.

I dial his office number, which was easier to find than his personal cell.

"Hello?" Davis answers.

"Hello. This is Detective Taylor with the Chicago Detective's Bureau."

"What is it now?" He breathes deeply into the phone with disgust.

Ignoring his unprofessionalism, I proceed, "I'm going to have to ask you to come in for a second interview, Mr. Parks."

"You're really not going to let me mourn my friend in peace, are you?"

"Are you going to come to the precinct, or do I need to come to you again?"

There's several seconds of silence. "I can come to you at 1 tomorrow," he grumbles.

"Perfect. I'll see you then." I hang up without giving him an opportunity to comment.

Now, it's time to return to the tedious job of reading Sullivan's emails. I pick up where I left off.

There's a quick double knock and then my office door creaks open.

I open my eyes to find my head resting on the keyboard. *I fell asleep!*

"Hiya, boss, I'm sorry to barge in like that. I uh—" Levi's standing in front of me stiffly.

"It is customary for people to be invited in after they knock." The irritation is resonating in my voice.

"I'm sorry. I just really thought you'd wanna know that I got into the phone. Since his email app was on his phone, I was able to trace the IP address for the Natalia woman. It traced back to a house in Sycamore, Illinois. It's a city a couple hours west of Chicago." He tears the sheet of paper with the address out of his notebook and passes it to me.

My hometown.

"I'm familiar with it." I stare at the barely legible handwriting.

"Do you want me to pass that information on to Ezra for you?"

"No, I'll let him know. Thank you, Levi. You've done well." I close the laptop and extend it to him. "Here. Take this and finish going through the emails. I left off on May 11th."

He faintly smiles and starts to leave. Then, he stops and turns back to me. "Ya know, there are people you can talk to if ya need to."

"I know. I appreciate that, Levi."

He leaves and closes the door behind him. Now, I have to fit in a road trip to Sycamore before my interview at 1 tomorrow.

14 January 2017
(32 Years Old)

Bartlett Cemetery Bartlett, Illinois

Snow is gently falling and blanketing the ground. The scene, as I approach the entrance to the cemetery, is peaceful and serene.

I walk slowly up the salted path to avoid slipping but also to read some of the headstones along the way. Some lived long, perhaps, happy lives, *1924–2012,* and others were gone too soon, *1980–1997.*

I see a familiar figure in the distance. He hasn't spotted me yet. His back is to me and his head bowed. Once I get within earshot, I announce my presence, "I don't remember this being such a long walk."

Ezra turns to me with a startled expression. "What're you doing here?"

"I stopped by your parents' house, and they told me I could find you here."

"That doesn't answer the question. What're you doing here?"

"You invited me, remember? Unless you ditching me at the pub was your way of withdrawing the invitation."

"Yeah. It kinda was. Besides, you're the one who said it would be unprofessional."

"I figured out a way around that."

"How's that?"

"I'm not staying overnight. I'm heading back to Chicago tonight."

"You really shouldn't have come here."

"Why not? I used to visit Benny's grave with you. You didn't have an issue then."

"Things were different then." The snow begins to fall heavily. Ezra turns away from me and stares off into the distance. A golf course runs parallel to the cemetery.

"I used to go golfing on that course with my dad and Benny," Ezra smiles as he shares this memory. "Me and Benny would place bets on our chores. Whoever lost had to do the other person's chores for a week."

"I'd always lose and it would make me so angry. That didn't stop me from betting with him though. He finally felt so bad for me that he let me win. I knew he let me but I didn't care."

Despite his smile, tears are streaming down his face when he turns to look at me again. "Have you ever had a bond like that with anyone, Mila?"

"No, I can't say I have. It's beautiful though. Thank you for sharing that memory with me."

"I should have many more memories to share. He should still be here." Ezra drops to his knees and buries his face in his hands.

I stoop down to rest a hand on his back. "It's not your fault. You know that, right? There's nothing you could've done to prevent what happened."

He uncovers his face to look up at me and states coldly, "He was seeing someone."

"He was what?" I step back.

"Yeah, I suspected that he was seeing someone. He was being really secretive about it."

"But you have no idea who."

"No idea. I should've asked more questions. It wasn't like him to keep things from me."

"Even if he was seeing someone, why is that bothering you? His killer is behind bars. Whoever he was seeing had nothing to do with his murder."

"Despite our conversation a couple weeks ago, you still don't get it." Ezra rises to his feet and takes a step in my direction. "Here, I'll spell it out for you. Benny's killer is still at large. I don't believe for one minute that Deek did it."

"You're just refusing to acknowledge all the evidence mounted against him, huh?"

"That isn't real evidence. All of it is circumstantial. Deek is such a low life. It didn't take a lot to frame him."

"Ezra, I'm saying this as a friend. You have to let this go for your own sanity. Benny's killer is behind bars. The sooner you accept that, the sooner you can make peace with what happened."

"Besides, do you really want to reopen this case and put yourself in a position to be treated as a suspect?"

"What's that supposed to mean?" Ezra growls.

"Think about it. You were the last person to see Benny alive. My point is either you accept that Deek is guilty or you open up a world of chaos for yourself. I can only protect you so much if the DA decides to pursue you as a suspect."

"It's time for you to go, Mila. I mean it. I don't want you here." He turns and walks in the opposite direction.

Taken aback by his sudden curtness, I momentarily consider going after him. Once the initial shock wears off and logic and reasoning kick in, I choose to respect his wishes and take the path back to the parking lot.

I've never heard Ezra address me so harshly. Nonetheless, I resolve not to follow him because I have a job to do and it doesn't involve catering to the feelings of others.

Present Day
10 October 2024

Sycamore, Illinois

"I'm heading to Sycamore to follow-up on a lead. You coming?" I say to Ezra as I'm standing over his desk.

He looks puzzled. "Your Sycamore?"

"Yes, are you coming?" I repeat.

He still looks like he's struggling to process what I'm asking before replying, "Yeah, just give me a few minutes to wrap something up. I'll meet you at your car."

I don't know if he's more confused about taking a trip to my hometown or about me inviting him to accompany me.

I brief him on the drive there. I detail my interview with Sullivan's dad, my encounter with the neighbor, Mr. Brewer, and my heated interview with Davis.

"Davis sounds suspicious. I should be in the interview with him tomorrow," Ezra remarks.

"You know I prefer to interview alone. It's less intimidating." I reach over and pat Ezra's knee. He flinches and pulls his leg away. *That's odd. He never used to mind it when I touched him.*

We ride the rest of the way in silence. I turn onto a neighborhood road lined with towering white oak and willow trees. It's not the same neighborhood I grew up in but there are similarities. All the houses look the same. One-story homes with about three feet of brick lining the base and perimeter. Beige siding extends from the brick to the roof. It's almost like the housing developers couldn't afford to build the whole house out of brick.

The asphalt road and driveways are faded and cracked. We've reached our destination. I turn into the driveway and shut off the car. The house is dark and we're the only car in the drive. Ezra and I give each other the same 'this doesn't look promising' look.

"Shall we?" I ask with uncertainty.

"Let's do it," he responds while opening his door.

There's a 'For Rent' sign in the yard and a lockbox on the front door. I test the windows on the front porch to see if any were left unlocked while Ezra walks around to the back. He comes back a few minutes later with no luck.

"The back door and windows are locked. I can't even get the window to the basement open," he reports.

"I'll call the agent on the 'For Rent' sign," I say while taking out my phone. "We'll have to wait for her to come let us in. This is a good thing. She should be able to tell us something about the previous tenant."

After I hang up with the agent, I fill Ezra in, "The agent's name is Simone Harper. I caught her at the perfect time. She's finishing an open house about 15 minutes from our location and she agreed to come meet with us."

"The only problem is she has made it clear that when it comes to her tenants, current or previous, she won't give out any of their confidential information without a search warrant or subpoena."

"Sometimes, our laws protect the wrong things and the wrong people." Ezra is aggravated and gets back in the passenger seat of the car to wait. I slide back into the driver's seat.

We're both lost in our own thoughts for a few minutes, when Ezra says, "Remember when we used to go undercover together?"

I smile.

He continues, "You used to wear that silly '70s looking wig."

"Hey, I like my brunette bob. I thought you did, too." I pretend to look upset.

"I prefer your stringy red hair." He flashes a playful grin.

"It's auburn."

"Oh, I'm sorry. I mean, stringy auburn hair."

I laugh and lightly jab his shoulder. This is the Ezra I miss. The one I could laugh with. The one who would tease me and I never got offended because I knew he was just being flirtatious.

"I still wear that wig. For undercover assignments, I mean." I point to the duffle bag in the back seat.

Ezra's eyes light up like a kid on Christmas morning. "You're kidding. It's in there? I have to see it." He reaches back and pulls the duffle bag into his lap. Before I can protest, he takes out the wig and puts it on his head. "How do I look?"

I can't contain my laughter. "It's not the most flattering for your features."

He looks at himself in the mirror and pretends like he's posing for a photo op.

"Alright," I interrupt. "That's enough fun with it. We need to put it back in the bag so it's still in good condition when I need it again."

"I think it's great that you still wear it." He chuckles as he places it back inside the duffle bag and carefully zips it up.

Our playful teasing makes the time pass quickly. This is exactly how we survived those endless hours of stakeouts. Before we know it, a tan SUV pulls up behind us. This must be Simone.

We exit the car and meet her on the sidewalk leading to the front door.

"I can let you into the house to look around but like I said before, I won't breach any client confidentiality agreements." Simone skips the introductions and gets right to the point. She's cooperating just enough to get us out of her hair.

I flash my badge. "I'm Detective Taylor and this is—" Ezra holds up his badge.

"I'm in a hurry. Do you want to see the house?" Simone cuts in.

"Aren't you the least bit curious about why we're here?" Ezra asks as we move toward the entrance.

Simone stops and turns to address Ezra, "I don't need to know but I'm not surprised either."

"What do you mean by that?" He counters.

"I mean, the previous tenant was shady. I didn't meet her in person, but she only signed a month-to-month lease and she paid in cash."

"When you say previous tenant, you mean Natalia, right?"

"Yes, Natalia." She stops abruptly.

"Natalia—" Ezra waits for Simone to supply a last name.

"Detective, I already told you. I refuse to disclose any personal information about my clients. If you're fishing for a last name, you're not going to get it from me."

"Can you explain how you never met her when you were her realtor and she paid in cash?"

"Well, let's see, background checks are done online. Applications are processed online. Leases are signed electronically. Payments can be dropped off in a deposit box after hours. Do I need to continue?" Simone replies snidely.

"We're in the 21st century, detectives. Also, I don't waste time connecting with my month-to-month tenants, especially when they tell me they're preparing to leave the country."

"Did she leave a forwarding address?" Ezra asks boldly.

"That's confidential and I've already said more than I planned." Simone gives Ezra the side eye and resumes walking. We follow close behind.

She punches a few numbers into the lockbox and releases the key. "Just lock up and put the key back in the lockbox when you're finished," she says as she hands the key to me.

"You're not staying?" Ezra really isn't picking up on Simone's complete indifference toward us and our investigation.

It's obvious to me that she's in a hurry to continue on with her day. I express our gratitude so she can be on her way. "Thank you, Ms. Harper. We appreciate your time and cooperation."

"Cooperation," Ezra sneers.

We both ignore him.

Simone is only addressing me now, "You're welcome. Thank you for understanding. I wish you luck in your investigation."

With that, she gives a frivolous wave and turns to walk away. In an instant, she pivots back to face us and adds, "I should warn you that our housekeeping team has already cleaned the place for the next tenant. They do an impeccable job. I'm really not sure what you're going to find in there." With that, she heads to her SUV.

Ezra stands forlornly on the porch after I've already unlocked and entered the house.

I call to Ezra from the foyer, "Come on, Ezra. Get over it. Simone Harper isn't a suspect. She did what she came here to do, which was to let us into the house."

He finally steps into the entryway. "I just remember a time when people were more helpful. A time when people weren't so wrapped up in their own lives and wouldn't hesitate to go the extra mile."

"What alternate reality did you live in?" I snap. "I don't ever remember a time when people sacrificed their own self-interests for the advancement of others."

"We did have very different childhoods." He looks at me like I'm a wounded dog. I reject his sympathy by looking away. Thankfully, he abandons mourning the death of his delusional worldview and he's ready to get back to work.

"You take the ground floor and I'll take the basement," he suggests.

We spend over an hour surveying every inch of the house. Fingerprints have been wiped clean. There's nothing left behind from the previous tenant, not even a hair or fiber of clothing.

Ezra and I meet back in the living room, empty-handed.

"What do we do now?" He sounds defeated again.

"You heard Simone. The previous tenant left the country. I think we're following a dead end here."

"So that's it? We drove all the way here just to give up?"

"Ezra, we're not giving up. We did our due diligence, so we can rule this Natalia woman out."

"Something's off. It doesn't sit right with me," he argues.

"What do you want me to do? If you want to interview every airline at O'Hare airport until you find out where she flew to and then fly across the world to interrogate her, be my guest. The woman broke things off and left months before his murder. I have suspects right here to focus on."

"Suspects? More than just Davis?" I've piqued his interest.

"Has anyone interviewed Sullivan's employees? He has so few social ties that as far I'm concerned, everyone he knew is a suspect. We need to find the person who last saw him alive." Ezra shrugs and has nothing to say because he knows I'm right.

As instructed, we lock up and put the key in the lockbox. Before I put the car in reverse, Ezra says something unexpected, "We should go see your childhood home."

I'm speechless.

"I'm no shrink but I think it'd be good for you," he explains.

"How do you figure?"

"Part of dealing with your past is returning to it and facing it head on."

"Since when did you become a trauma expert?" I jab.

"Since I forced myself to reckon with my own trauma. I've gone back to the alley where Benny was found numerous times. So many times, I've built a small memorial for him there."

"Let me get this straight. You want me to go up to the door of my childhood home and build a memorial where my sister was killed?"

"Don't be ridiculous, Mila. Of course not. I do think you should go inside though."

"What do I tell the current tenants? My sister died here. Can I come inside?" I laugh.

Ezra is far from amused. "We'll think of an excuse when we get there. Let's just go."

"I don't even remember how to get there," I lie as I back out of the driveway.

In less than ten minutes, we're parked outside my childhood home. The weeping willow in the center of the yard is just as massive as I remember it to be. I loved that tree growing up.

I remember scaling the trunk and perching on its strong branches. I'd bring a book or a journal with me and stay up there for hours. My dad and Farah never thought to look for me there. Either that or they just didn't care when I disappeared.

"Do you want me to come in with you?" Ezra asks gently.

"No, I need to do this on my own," I say with strength.

At the front door, I knock confidently. A middle-aged woman with long, full auburn hair opens the door. She's wearing a light pink cardigan and blue jeans.

She looks surprised and opens her mouth to say something when I cut her off, "Hello, ma'am. I apologize for the intrusion. My name is Detective Taylor." I flash my badge. "May I come inside to ask a few questions?"

The woman looks concerned and nods. I hastily step inside. As soon as I close the front door behind me, a huge smile spreads across my face.

The middle-aged woman laughs and says, "You had me worried there for a second. I thought my sister was really here to arrest me or somethin'. What are you doing here? We weren't expecting you here until Saturday."

"I'm in town on some detective business and just wanted to stop in for a quick visit. I'm still coming Saturday. You know I'm not gonna miss Sydney's first varsity volleyball game." I flop down on the couch in the living room.

Farah goes over to the living room window and peeks through the blinds. "Who's that? He's cute." She tries to wave to Ezra but he's looking down at his phone. "Can I go out and meet him?"

"He may be cute but he's not the kind of person I want to introduce to my family."

Farah turns to look at me. She seems perturbed. "You've been working for the police department for, what, twenty years now and I've never met anyone you work with.

You never invite me to Chicago to see where you live or work. I'm beginning to think you're a secret agent or somethin'."

I laugh. "Farah, come on now. You know Chicago is no place for Sydney to visit. It's not safe there. Maybe when she's a little older, we can plan a trip for you guys to come see me."

"Mila, she's sixteen. Don't you think she's old enough?"

I look at my watch. "I've gotta get going. This was just supposed to be a pit stop. We can talk more about it this weekend."

I jump up and give Farah a quick embrace. "I'll let myself out. Tell Sydney I can't wait for Saturday!"

"Ok, love you," Farah says as she watches me leave the house as quickly as I came in.

I walk briskly to the car. I pretend to be flustered as I turn the car on and put it in gear. Once I pull away from the house, Ezra probes me for answers, "So?"

"So what?" My voice sounds bothered.

"How did it go?"

"How do you think it went? It was terrible. I really don't want to talk about it."

"That bad, huh? I'm sorry I pressured you," Ezra says solemnly. "When you're ready to talk about it, I'm here."

"It's not your fault. You didn't make me do anything. I just wasn't ready." I pause and then add, "Thank you for caring though."

I reach over and grab Ezra's hand. This time, he doesn't pull away.

There have been many occasions on which I've come close telling Ezra the truth about Farah. Today was one of them. I would've liked to introduce Farah to Ezra. They're two of my favorite people.

I've regretted the lie since the day I told it but not enough to bring myself to come clean. About a month after we were assigned as partners, which was a few months after Benny's death, Ezra and I were on an hours-long stakeout when he opened up about Benny's death.

He shared his grief, his anger, his hatred. It was such a raw conversation. Before I knew it, I was telling him about my childhood trauma. I told him about the day I skipped school and overheard the heated argument between my dad and Farah, except I changed one major detail.

In that moment, I craved sympathy and I wasn't going to get it by telling what really happened. Once I spun the lie, there was no turning back in my mind. What's harder than telling the lie is keeping it straight.

8 June 2002
(18 Years Old)

Sycamore, Illinois Graduation Day

Today is the first day of the rest of my life, at least that's what my high school's valedictorian said during our graduation ceremony this morning. My life has been a series of uncertainties ever since Dad's arrest.

Since then, I've watched a judge commit my dad to a mental institution. I've waited by my sister's bedside, wondering if she'll ever wake up from a coma. The whole time I was under the delusion that if and when she woke up, we would be reunited and able to live together again.

To my dismay, when Farah woke up, I stayed in a foster home and Farah was placed in a long-term care facility. The swelling in her brain stem caused deficits in her language and fine motor skills.

She had to relearn how to speak in complete sentences, how to walk, and how to do everyday things like holding utensils to eat or a pencil to write. It was a long, slow two-year road for Farah.

In a strange way, I was jealous of her. While she had to learn to live again, she didn't have any recollection of the events that occurred on the day her injuries were inflicted. I, on the other hand, replay that day in my mind constantly.

During her stay, Farah and one of the young, handsome interns at the facility fell in love. Some of the doctors and nurses found it unethical, so the young man took an internship at a different facility but continued to visit and court Farah until her release.

The day she was released, Farah and Curtis were married at the Justice of the Peace with me as the witness. I had no interest in dating or marriage but found myself envious of Farah yet again.

I was bounced around to multiple foster homes as she fell into the arms of her husband. Jaded is an understatement for how I felt when Farah and Curtis didn't invite me to live with them.

My fourteen-year-old mind didn't understand that as a young couple, neither with college degrees, they couldn't afford to take care of me and could barely afford to take care of themselves.

Curtis was in college, pursuing a medical degree, so rather than having Farah endure the mental and financial stress of getting her GED and starting college, they decided she would stay home and, when the time is right, she would take care of their children.

Another factor that played into the decision was Farah's disability. Farah's fine motor skills improved before being released from long-term care but never fully returned to normal. A job as a waitress or anything that required keen hand-eye-coordination was out of the question.

Farah was living a new life with her husband while I was being kicked out of a third foster home. I was kicked out of the first one when the parents found out about my dad. Something about housing the child of a violent man committed to a mental institution freaked them out.

The day they dropped me back off at social services, I vividly remember the foster dad saying in a low voice, "I know where the darkness within her comes from," to the social worker.

Neither the mom nor the dad looked at me as they walked out. Despite being complete strangers, the rejection I endured was indescribable.

The second foster home was equally unsuccessful. This time, the foster parents, Mr. and Mrs. Clayton, brought me back to social services because their teenage son developed a crush on me, which, according to them, was my fault for tempting him.

One day, when I was making a peanut butter and jelly sandwich in the kitchen after school, their son, Jonas, joined me unexpectedly. I had lived in their house for three months and this was the first time he had spoken to me.

He asked if he could have a sandwich, too. I gave him the one I was making and made another one. From there, a friendship blossomed. Jonas was two years older than me, so we didn't talk at school. But at home, we made it a ritual to meet in the kitchen for a peanut butter and jelly.

After that, we either played video games or did our homework together. It didn't take long for his mom to take notice of our friendship and she didn't condone it. Mrs. Clayton was passive aggressive about it and would interfere with our hangout time by sending Jonas to do chores, leaving him little to no time to hang out with me.

The night before I was brought back to social services, Mrs. Clayton caught Jonas sneaking out of my room. Earlier that day, Jonas and I had tried to meet up in the kitchen for our after-school sandwich, when his mom conveniently showed up with a long list of chores.

This was the longest list I had seen her give him yet. It made me feel like it was my fault he was being punished. By selfishly holding onto our friendship against his mom's will, I was giving her reason to take control of all his free time.

As Jonas diligently worked through the list of chores, I came to terms with the only way to rectify the situation. I would tell Jonas that we can no longer be friends. Mrs. Clayton made sure that I didn't have any time to talk to him that day though.

Jonas had never snuck into my room before. I was lying in bed, staring at the ceiling, when I heard my door creak open. I shot out of bed but relaxed when I heard his familiar voice.

"Shhh. Mila," Jonas whispers. "I just wanna talk." He quietly closes the door behind him.

I sit down on the edge of the bed and whisper, "Same."

"You go first." Jonas sits next to me.

"This is really hard for me to say." I pause.

"I really like you," Jonas blurts.

I was not expecting that. I'm speechless, so he says, "That isn't what you were going to say, is it?"

"No," I say softly. "I was going to say that we need to stop being friends, for your sake."

"For my sake?"

"Yes. Jonas, it's clear that your mom has an issue with our friendship. She's going to keep punishing you with chore after chore after chore until we're no longer friends. It's not worth it."

"That's your opinion. I think it's worth it. It kinda hurts that you don't." Jonas stands and looks at me. I think the realization is setting in. I don't have the same feelings he does.

"Look, I'm not good for you. Believe me. You'll thank me later." The coldness in my tone even takes me by surprise.

Jonas is noticeably in shock. I don't know what he thought the outcome of our conversation would be but this was not it. He turns away from me and walks to the door. After opening it, he looks at me one final time and leaves without a word. On the other side of the door, he finds his mom waiting.

The next morning, I wake up to Mrs. Clayton packing my things. It was Wednesday and I was supposed to be getting ready for school but instead, I was rejected and displaced once again. Jonas stayed in his room as my belongings were loaded into the Clayton's car and I was driven away.

After that, I managed to stay in my third home for nearly two years. That was the longest stint yet. The reason for being kicked out this time was not nearly as interesting or exciting as the others.

My foster dad got a job offer in another state and he and his wife decided to take it. Part of me hoped they'd take me with them, not because I wanted to be adopted or because I was attached to them. But because I was tired and yearned for stability.

Three different families, all with different dynamics. I didn't want to get to know any more families and their dysfunctional ways.

Here I am today. Somehow, I survived a fourth home, a fourth school and managed to graduate. My fourth home brought more promise than the previous ones. I don't have foster parents but a foster mom.

She's a kind-hearted and sweet elderly woman named Ms. Trudy Prewitt. She asked me to call her Trudy and treated me like family the moment I entered her home. Trudy is widowed and childless.

Her husband died while on active duty before they could begin a family. She was never able to love another and devoted her life to helping foster children.

I'm eighteen now. Therefore, Trudy has no obligation to continue to help me but she's insisting that I stay with her through the summer. In the fall, I'll head to Aurora University to study criminal justice.

For the first time in years, I can honestly say it's going to be hard to leave. In the short time I've lived with Trudy, she's helped me get my life back on track. I'm genuinely going to miss her.

Farah and Curtis didn't attend my graduation today. In their defense, they weren't invited either. This has nothing to do with them not taking me in a few years ago. It's quite the opposite.

After Curtis graduated with a nursing degree, they finally had enough money to buy a house and start a family.

Farah noticed that our childhood home was up for sale and she convinced Curtis to buy it. I couldn't believe it.

How could she not only go back there, but live there? They invited me to live with them and I refused. I would rather live in twenty foster homes than step foot in that house again.

Farah just kept saying that it reminds her of Mom and her memories are not as tainted as mine. Maybe someday I'll be willing to go to that house but I'm just not there yet.

Present Day
11 October 2024

Sully's Read n Sip W. Madison St.

I wake up, feeling well-rested for the first time in months. As soon as my head hit the pillow last night, I was out. I slept like a baby. There's no way to predict when the sleepless nights will ensue.

On the rare occasion that I do get a good night's sleep, I naively believe that this is the start of a new and healthy pattern. Within a day or two, I'm right back to lying awake at night, beseeching rest that never comes.

It's still early. If I get ready now, I can make it to *Sully's Read n Sip* before my interview with Davis at 1. James or one of the other employees should be there. When I dropped Ezra off last night, he said it's still open.

This comes as no surprise. With Davis still owning a portion of the business, he must've chosen to keep its doors open until he can decide the fate of the cafe.

There's a slight chill in the air as I walk up the sidewalk on W. Madison. I pass Sullivan's apartment building and continue on until I reach the bookstore and cafe. Through the giant windows, I see layers of bookcases with neatly shelved books.

When I reach the entrance, I pull open the massive door and enter the cafe. On my right, there's an older gentleman reading a book, one purchased here presumably, as he sips a cup of coffee and nibbles on a blueberry scone. The shop smells of freshly brewed coffee and the pages of old books.

This place really is warm and inviting. I see why Sullivan couldn't let it go.

I can picture myself getting lost in a book as I caffeinate and indulge in a pastry. Straight ahead, there's a man in his mid to late 20s watching me from behind a counter. As I draw closer, his name tag comes into focus. *James.*

"You're not here for a book or for a coffee, are you?" James shifts uneasily from one foot to the other.

"Unfortunately, no." I know an answer wasn't truly necessary, but I want James to feel comfortable.

"What can I do for you then?" James asks earnestly.

I hold up my badge, followed by the usual introduction.

"I know this is difficult for you, Mr.—" I search his badge for a last name.

"Freeman," he offers.

"Mr. Freeman, I just need to ask you a few questions."

James is anxious but he's willing to cooperate. I pull my tape recorder out of my bag and the interview gets underway.

"When was the last time you saw Sullivan Maxwell alive, Mr. Freeman?" I begin.

James' eyes dim as he stares off. "Here. I worked the closing shift that night, the last night he was alive. Sometimes, I think I still see him, round a bookshelf or sitting at one of the cafe tables."

A tear rolls down James' cheek and gets caught in his beard. He doesn't bother to wipe it away. I know this is one of many tears he's shed for his late-boss.

"Would you describe Mr. Maxwell as a fair employer?"

"Sullivan Maxwell was not just an employer. He was a loyal friend. He was family." James' tone reveals he's offended.

I dial back, "I'll take that as he was a fair employer. How wonderful to have been able to know him and have him in your life for so long. You are the longest employee here, am I right?"

"That's correct. I was in high school when I started here. This was only supposed to be a temporary job but I quickly fell in love with the place. Sullivan made it hard not to. He made me feel valued and never treated me like an inexperienced kid even when I was one."

"He taught me everything he knew about business. He wanted to help me launch my own but I've just never been ready to leave."

"Did you know that Davis Parks never sold his shares of the business?"

"Not until recently." Beads of sweat appear on his forehead.

"What are you anxious about, Mr. Freeman?"

"Please, call me James." He wipes his forehead with a napkin. "I don't want to get anyone in trouble."

"No one will be in trouble unless there's good reason for them to be in trouble."

Before resuming, James pours himself a cup of water and chugs it. He offers me a cup and I decline.

He's finally ready to continue. "That night, the last night I saw Sully, we were stocking books and having a casual conversation, nothing out of the ordinary, when Tabitha showed up."

"Tabitha Parks? What time was this?"

"Yes, Tabitha Parks. It was around 8, almost closing time. She came in on a rampage, ranting and raving about Davis still owning his shares and she just found out about it after all these years."

"Luckily, it was almost closing time and the shop was empty because she was causing a real scene. She aired out all of Sully's business in front of me. That woman has no shame or compassion."

"What do you mean by business?"

"Sullivan fell behind in the mortgage for this place. He also owed two years of back taxes. He had been evading the IRS for quite some time. That's how Tabitha found out. The mortgage company and the IRS started coming after Davis."

"You didn't know about any of this?"

"I promise I had no idea. Sully handled all the financial stuff. He was very particular about that kind of thing."

Now, we know why. He wasn't much of a businessman, was he?

"How did Sullivan handle the situation with Tabitha?"

"He asked me if I could lock up on my own and then convinced Tabitha to walk outside with him."

"Where outside?"

"They didn't get far, just right outside that window." James points to one of the large windows I was looking into when I walked up. "They stopped there and started arguing. I was watching them from behind a bookshelf."

"They were both shouting but it was too muffled to make out what was said. Tabitha was waving her hands wildly and then—"

I lean in.

"She slaps him. Hard."

The scratch on Sullivan's cheek.

"Sullivan stood there with his hand to his cheek and Tabitha marched off like she'd won some kind of battle. He looked over in my direction, but I don't think he saw me. I was pretty well hidden."

"I keep replaying what happened next in my mind. He slowly walked down the sidewalk toward his apartment building. I watched him until he disappeared out of view. I wish I had gone out to him, checked on him. Maybe he'd still be here. I hate that the last time I saw him, he was hurting, and I did nothing."

"You had no way of knowing that you wouldn't see him again. Did you actually see him go into his apartment building?"

"No, I didn't watch him any further than what I could see through that window."

"Is the altercation with Tabitha the reason why you called Davis to notify him of Sullivan's death?"

"No. Remember, I was here when this was *M&P's Read n Sip*. Davis and I have stayed in touch over the years. I've spent a few holidays with his family because mine is far away. I was kind of hurt when I learned that he was keeping this huge secret from me though."

"Why do you think Sullivan and Davis kept it from you?"

"With all due respect, Detective, I don't want to speculate. You'll have to ask Davis that one."

"I respect that. As a matter of fact, I'm meeting with him in a couple hours."

All the blood drained from James' face in an instant. "Are you going to tell him what I said about his wife? About her showing up here like that? Please don't. He's my employer and I need this job."

"What makes you think Davis will keep this place?"

"I don't know if he will but I need this job until I can find a new one."

"I won't mention that we spoke. How does that sound?"

The color returns to James' face. "Thank you. You have no idea how relieved I am to hear that."

James doesn't realize how it will work to my advantage to withhold this information from Davis. This way, I can catch him in so many lies.

"Is there anything else, any other details, from your last encounter with Sullivan that you're able to share?"

"That's all I've got, Detective. Can you do me one other favor though?"

"What's that?"

"Remember that he was a good man and didn't deserve this. He had his flaws and lapses in judgment like every other human being. He was one of the best humans I've ever had the privilege of knowing." James gets choked up and turns away from me, so I stop recording.

"Thank you for your time, James. I truly am appreciative. Here's my card. Please contact me if you think of anything else that will help this investigation."

James doesn't reach for the card because he's holding his face in the palms of his hands as he sobs quietly. I lay my card on the counter and exit the way I came.

The poor guy is going to be lost without Sullivan.

Thanksgiving Day, 2008 (24 Years Old)

Sycamore, Illinois

The year I visited Dad at Chester was the year Sydney was born. Up till that point, I kept my word to not set foot in that old house. If Farah wanted to catch up with me, I met her at a restaurant or coffee shop in Sycamore.

She would spend the first half of our visit fuming with me for declining her invitation to come to her house for the holidays. Sydney changed things for me. When I met her in the hospital, before Farah and Sydney were discharged, I absolutely fell in love with her.

Her little fingers and toes, her sweet smell, and her tiny button nose were too much to resist. I cuddled her for hours that day. Only giving her back to allow Farah to feed her. To be clear, in no way did it trigger a desire to have a family of my own. It did, however, give me further motivation to create a world that was safer for Sydney to grow up in than the one I experienced.

I can smell the mouth-watering aromas of turkey roasting and pumpkin pie baking as I stand on the doorstep of Farah's home. When Farah asked me to bring a few side dishes, I was relieved to discover that the nearby grocery store was advertising ready-made Thanksgiving sides. Farah should understand that since I've only ever had to cook for myself, I never truly learned to cook. I'm really doing them a favor by picking up the sides as opposed to trying to make them myself.

I'm juggling a few grocery bags when Curtis opens the door. He frowns when he sees the bags in my hand but still reaches out in a weak attempt to assist me.

He's judging me for bringing store bought sides. I knew he would.

I twist my body to move the bags away from his grasping hand.

"No, thank you. I've got this," I say as I move past him.

Curtis and I aren't particularly fond of each other. When I met Farah out at restaurants, she would make excuses for why Curtis couldn't make it but I knew the real reason. He's never liked me.

It upset him that I wasn't happy for Farah when they found each other years ago. It angered him that I refused to come to their house for so many years. Not because he wanted to see me but because he saw the distress it caused Farah.

I'm not saying his reasons are wrong or invalid. I can admit that I've been selfish. I'm also not afraid to admit that I could care less about how Curtis feels about me. When Farah met him, I couldn't understand how she could trust a man so easily after what we went through with our dad.

Farah's entirely too forgiving and too accepting. That's another reason why I need to be around for my niece. I don't want Sydney to grow up to be as gullible and naive as her mother.

"Happy Thanksgiving," I add as I head to the kitchen without turning to look at him.

He doesn't respond and I'm okay with that. As I enter the kitchen, the first person I see is my beautiful baby niece snuggled in her swing near the kitchen table. She's contentedly kicking her feet as she looks up at the colorful toys dangling in front of her. I drop the bags on the island and rush to her.

"There's my pretty girl!" I gush as I crouch down in front of her. She continues to kick her tiny feet and makes giddy noises.

Farah laughs as she removes the warm sides from the grocery bags and lines them up on the counter. "I should've known you wouldn't actually cook anything."

I stand and walk over to the sides. "Who needs to cook, when you can pick up steamy mashed potatoes, already seasoned and cooked green beans, and your favorite," I pull the lid off the side closest to me and gesture like Vanna White, "creamy mac n cheese?"

Farah walks over and wraps her arms around me. "You know I don't really care about the sides, right? I'm just glad you're here."

"Happy Thanksgiving, Farah," I whisper as I give her a tight squeeze in return.

"Happy Thanksgiving, Sis," she whispers back.

After pulling away, I go about helping Farah by setting the table and when Sydney starts fussing, I take her out of the swing and carry her around to give Farah a break.

I can tell Curtis is avoiding the kitchen while I'm in here, so I carry Sydney out to the living room. Just as suspected, as soon as I exit the kitchen, Curtis goes in to finish up the turkey.

I don't let his childish behavior bother me. Rather, I become preoccupied with admiring the changes to the decor. Other than the layout, Farah and Curtis have done a fantastic job of transforming this house to look nothing like our childhood home.

They ripped out that awful brown paneling in the living room and painted the walls a pastel green with white trim. The beer-stained carpet was removed and hardwood flooring took its place. They even installed a ceiling fan with soft white lighting.

I walk over and stare at the spot where I believe the violent act occurred years ago. I imagine Farah's teenage body crumpled, lying lifeless on the floor. Blood pooling on the carpet from the head wound.

I wonder if that's the real reason they had the carpet removed. Sydney whimpers, causing me to break free from my trance. She wants me to keep moving, so I walk around the living room a few times while gently rocking her.

Her eyes begin to close and I take this opportunity to sit on the edge of the cushy beige sofa. I look down at her and watch her drift off to sleep. Then I say softly, "Don't worry, baby girl. Auntie Mila will always be here to protect you."

Present Day
11 October 2024

Bureau of Detectives, Forensic Services Division

When I arrive at the bureau thirty minutes prior to the interview, Davis is waiting for me.

"Mr. Parks, nice to see you again. Thank you for being so punctual," I greet him with a friendly smile and a handshake.

Davis mumbles something unintelligible and then responds, "I have business in the city. If we could make this as quick as possible, I'd appreciate it."

"Oh, you must mean selling the company you never actually sold years ago," I state matter-of-factly.

The color drains from Davis' face. There's fear in his eyes. He knows it wasn't a question and the cat's out of the bag. Rather than digging a deeper hole, he chooses to follow me silently to my office.

He sits in a chair across from me as I sit behind my desk, the tape recorder between us. A look of dread written all over his face. I can tell he's regretting agreeing to a second interview. I'm surprised he doesn't refuse to answer any more questions without a lawyer present.

It's almost as if he knows what I'm thinking because he says, "I have nothing to hide. Let's get this over with."

I'm already recording, so I have no issue jumping right to the purpose of this interview. "Mr. Parks, please explain why your name is on last year's tax documents for *Sully's Read n Sip?"*

"Isn't it obvious? I never sold my portion of the company. That isn't a crime, Detective." Davis leans back and crosses his arms arrogantly.

"No, that isn't a crime but withholding pertinent information from a homicide investigation is. Let's not make this harder than it needs to be. Explain why your name is on last year's tax documents."

Davis exhales deeply in discontent. "When I approached Sully about selling my shares of the company back in 2017, he begged me not to. He said he didn't have enough money to buy them from me and bringing in a stranger could ruin our vision."

"I couldn't just abandon my friend, so we made a deal. I agreed not to sell as long as Sully kept it under wraps and I no longer had any financial obligations. I let Sully keep all the profits and in return, he didn't come to me asking for any money."

"Who did you have to keep it a secret from?"

"Tabitha. She would've never married me if I refused to sell. She was convinced the company would cause us hardship and prevent us from the life she pictured for us. Sully and I had to pretend to be estranged, so Tabby wouldn't be suspicious."

"Eventually, it wasn't an act anymore. Without me at the shop to help out, we drifted apart and stopped talking altogether. I know Sully still felt abandoned. I was absent when he needed me the most."

"Does Tabitha know now?"

"No, she doesn't have the slightest idea. That's why I need to discuss things with James today."

So, he doesn't know about the altercation with Tabitha.

"Why James? He's just an employee. What influence does he have on what happens to the company?"

"Oh, you don't know?" Davis laughs haughtily.

"Know what?"

"Sully left his half of the company to James in his will." Davis grins mischievously. *He really thinks he's going to take the attention off him and put it on James.*

I keep a straight face.

Why didn't James mention this to me though?

"What do you plan to do then?"

"I want out. I know James won't be able to buy my shares, so I'm gonna offer to gift them to him. If the company tanks afterwards, that's not my problem. I don't owe James the way I owed Sully."

"Why didn't you just gift it to Sully in the first place?"

"I convinced myself that it wasn't total abandonment if I remained as a stakeholder. I think part of me hoped to be able to return and work with him again someday, even if it was after retirement from my corporate job. All foolish thinking and foolish choices at this point."

"Where were you around 8 on the night of October 5th?"

"Home with Tabitha and the kids." Davis' pupils dilate and his eyes shift.

He's lying. Tabitha was at the bookstore. Why is he covering for her? Unless, he wasn't home either.

"Can Tabitha confirm your alibi?"

"Yes." We stare at each other for several seconds, waiting for the other to flinch. "Why do I need an alibi? Am I a suspect now?" Davis asks after he finally looks away.

"Everyone is a suspect right now, Mr. Parks."

"Then, you should do your job and investigate James, Detective. He's the only one who had a reason to kill Sully. James is the only one who had anything to gain from his death."

"That's still up for debate." I shouldn't poke at the bull, but Davis is such a pompous prick, it's difficult to resist.

"I have a question for you, Detective."

"What's that?"

"Was the New Year's Eve in the bar years ago, the last time you spoke to Sullivan?"

"I apologize but I don't know what you're referring to."

"You thought I wouldn't remember you? Pretty lady at the bar, ditched by her co-worker?"

"I'm flattered, but you're mistaken, Mr. Parks." *You're not going to turn this around on me.*

Davis doesn't look like he wants to let this go. He's having a mental battle but his urgent business in the city prevails.

"If you don't have any further questions, then I really need to get going," he barks.

"I don't have any further questions at this time. You're free to go, Mr. Parks."

Immediately after stopping the recorder, Davis stands and walks out of my office, without a concluding remark or even a parting gesture.

I don't have time to concern myself with his crudeness. I need to make it to the Parks' house in Aurora to interview Tabitha before Davis gets home. Either, he knows something and is covering for her or he wasn't home either and hopes to use her as an alibi. I grab my keys, handbag, Kitty Charm jacket and head to my car.

12 July 2013
(29 Years Old)

My Apartment N. Clark St.

I'm supposed to spend the weekend in Sycamore at Farah's but something's come up.

"Hello?" Farah answers after the second ring. I hear the kitchen sink running and Sydney chatting in the background.

"Mama, can I eat this?" Sydney asks hopefully. I imagine her holding up a snack-size bag of crackers. Sydney loves her snacks.

"No, Syd. Dinner's almost ready. Are you on your way here, Mila?"

"That's why I'm calling. I can't make it this weekend."

"What? Why? We've been planning this for weeks." Farah doesn't try to hide her disappointment.

"I'm sorry. It's work. You know I wouldn't cancel unless I absolutely had to," I lie. I can't tell her the real reason for canceling. She wouldn't understand.

Farah sighs heavily. "I hate your job. Not only is it dangerous work but now, it's interfering with family time."

"Okay, Mom," I respond playfully. "I'll tell my boss that I need to be home for dinner tonight."

"I'm serious, Mila. It's not right how they call you into work at the last minute and constantly expect you to put your life on the line."

"It's what I signed up for, Farah. I thought you'd be proud."

"I hope you're not doing this for me," Farah rebukes. "I'd prefer for you to have a safe desk job. I don't like having to worry about getting a call that my little sister has been killed in the line of duty."

You won't get a call. They don't even know you exist.

Now, I'm getting irked. "This is what I've chosen to do with my life and I need you to get over it."

Farah's silent. She doesn't like it when I snap at her but her constant worry for my safety has become tiresome.

"I really need to get going, so I'll call you later, okay?" There's a long pause and I wonder if Farah has hung up. "Hello, Farah?"

"Okay," she reluctantly answers.

"Thank you. Love you. Please tell Syd Auntie Mila loves her, too."

"You can tell her when you see her," Farah replies immaturely. Then, she relaxes her tone and adds, "Be careful, Mila."

"Always."

We both say goodbye and hang up. I touch up my makeup and smooth out my hair. It's almost time to head out.

I'm meeting a guy named Benny from the precinct for a casual drink. We were both in line to file paperwork the other day when he slipped me a piece of paper, asking if I'd go on a date with him sometime. It was cute in that middle school crush kind of way.

I agreed to meet him out tonight but under the pretense that no one else knows. It didn't take any convincing because he isn't ready for his twin brother, who's also his partner in the force, to know. We're even going as far as to meet in Schaumburg, about 30 minutes outside of Chicago.

Farah doesn't need to know either. It's just a casual meet-up. There's no sense in getting his brother and my sister involved. We're not planning a wedding. We're just having a drink.

I give my outfit one final check in the mirror. I hardly recognize myself when I'm out of my patrol uniform. Ripped jeans hug my hips and a loose-fitting V-neck compliments my neckline. Will Benny be just as attracted to me in jeans and a t-shirt as he is in my blues?

Don't make this a bigger deal than it really is. Remember, no attachments.

Present Day
11 October 2024

Aurora, Illinois

On the long drive to the Parks' house, I give Ezra a call.

"Hello," he answers.

"Hey, I was just wondering if there have been any matches to the print found on the mug since the last time I checked."

"No, still no match. We've run it through the criminal and civil databases every day, twice a day." There's a pause. "Where are you?"

Why is he always asking about my whereabouts? It's really none of his business.

"How do you know I'm not in my office? It's like you have my location or something." I laugh.

He doesn't find it funny.

"I can hear the humming of the engine in the background. It's a simple question. Stop being so difficult. Where are you?"

"I'm heading back to the Parks' house," I humor him.

"What? Why? Didn't you just interview Davis Parks right here in the precinct?" Ezra sounds so confused and I'm enjoying it.

"Yes. Some information he shared or should I say, didn't share, about Tabitha is making her look like a suspect. He lied about her whereabouts on the night of Sullivan's murder."

There's something electrifying about having information that no one else does and even more thrilling to be the one to disclose that information. I might add, especially when you're disclosing it to someone who thinks he's always been a better detective than you.

"I don't think she did it," Ezra says smugly.

"Why is that?"

"Full disclosure, I'm still following this Natalia character. I know a guy in the FBI. He's saying Natalia doesn't exist."

"Oh! You know a guy in the FBI, and that's supposed to halt my end of the investigation? Ezra knows a guy, everyone. His findings are the only ones that matter."

I realize how childish I must sound and change my angle. "So, Sullivan was communicating with an imaginary person?" It sounds sarcastic but I'm asking earnestly.

"No, of course not. There's a real person but her name's not Natalia."

"What's her name then?" I ask coolly.

"I don't know the answer to that question yet but I'm working on it."

"Well, you keep following that dead end and I'll go interview a real suspect."

"I hope you're right."

"What was that?"

"I hope you're right. I hope I never find out who Natalia really is."

I think I know what he means but I don't ask. He thinks Natalia is connected to Benny's murder, too. I'm not going to entertain his conspiracy theories. I've already tried to persuade him to let this go. Since I'm pulling into the Parks' neighborhood, we end the call.

When I pull into the driveway at the Parks' house, Tabitha appears on the sidewalk next to the driveway. She must've seen me through the living room window.

She's waving her hands back and forth and shaking her head as she says something to me. Her angry words are muffled because my windows are up and my music is still on.

I turn off the car and proceed to get out. She meets me at my car door. Her behavior is a little erratic.

"Davis isn't here. You need to leave now," she barks as she moves closer to me.

"Whoa." I hold up my hands to warn her to back off. "I'm not here to speak to Davis. I'm here to speak to you."

Like a small dog, her bark is worse than her bite. Tabitha backs off with an alarmed expression on her face.

"Why do you need to talk to me?" She shrinks back and her aggressive behavior diminishes.

"You were one of the last people to see Sullivan alive." I allow silence to fill the space between us.

After the initial shock wears off, Tabitha sits down crisscross on her driveway, buries her face in her hands and cries.

This is a first.

I've never had a witness or a suspect sit down on the ground and cry. If sympathy is what she's looking for with these antics, she's not going to get it from me. The fact that she's crying, tells me what James said is true. Now, she owes me an explanation as to why she withheld this information from the police.

I close my car door and lean against it, waiting for Tabitha to pull herself together. Her cries begin to subside, and she looks at me with mascara streaming down her face.

"Are you here to arrest me?" Before I can answer, her bottom lip quivers and she buries her face in her hands again.

"Is there something I need to arrest you for?" With how rude she's been to me, I'm enjoying this power I have over her right now.

"I didn't kill Sullivan," she sobs without looking up at me.

"Then it shouldn't be difficult to explain why you didn't tell anyone about seeing him that night."

Tabitha looks up at me with hatred in her eyes. "You know I didn't just see him. I know how it looks. I know James heard me yelling at Sully. I know he saw me slap him. Don't you think for one second that I don't know how that looks?"

There's that feisty woman I'm familiar with. She feels backed into a corner and now, she's ready to fight her way out.

"How does it look?"

"It looks like I k—" she couldn't choke the word out this time.

"Killed him? You know what looks even more suspicious? The fact that you had an altercation with him that night and tried to hide it." I'm still casually leaning against my car door, unamused by Tabitha's ridiculous behavior.

Tabitha must realize in that moment that she looks like a crazy woman because she pulls herself to her feet and brushes off her pants. She attempts to wipe the tears and mascara off her face with her hands.

My window is down, so I reach into my car to grab a box of tissues and toss it to her. Tabitha clenches the box with one hand while pulling a few tissues out with the other and tosses the box back to me.

She doesn't even bother to say thank you. She wipes her face and then blows her nose. She still looks like a wreck.

Her voice is shaky as she asserts, "I was scared. I still am. I have a family to protect. I lost my temper that night and I'm ashamed of the way I acted. I feel terrible about the way I treated Sullivan."

"He didn't deserve that. The fact that the altercation, or whatever you called it, is the last memory he had of me haunts me. But I did not kill him."

At this point, I realize that I haven't recorded any of this encounter. I know if I ask, Tabitha will refuse, so I'm going to have to continue without any evidence of this interview. It will be Tabitha's word against mine if she decides to change her story later on.

"Why is Davis covering for you?" I ask pointedly.

"Huh? What do you mean? Covering for me?" Tabitha is genuinely confused.

"I have him on record saying that you were home with him at 8 on the night of October 5th," I explain.

Tabitha's mouth gapes open. "Why would he do that?" She gasps.

"So, you realize that I have your husband on record lying to the police about your whereabouts." It's not a question.

"Surly, you don't think I murdered Sullivan and convinced my husband to cover for me," Tabitha declares with a horrified look on her face.

"That's how it appears. Unless—"

"Unless what?"

"Unless Davis doesn't have an alibi either. Where was he on the night Sullivan was murdered?"

"He was home with our kids. I can supply doorbell camera footage to prove that he ordered pizza that night. It was delivered around 7:30. The footage shows him accepting the pizza from the delivery driver. He goes back inside and never leaves again."

I can tell Tabitha has been preparing for this very moment. The moment she needs to protect and defend Davis. She must've known that it was only a matter of time before James ratted her out.

"What time did you get home that night?" I inquire.

"It was late and it looks bad for me. After I slapped Sully, I got in my car and I drove. I drove for about 20 minutes and found myself driving back to *Sully's Read n Sip*. I felt terrible."

"I wasn't ready to face Davis. I knew I would have to tell him what I did. He was going to be so upset with me and for good reason. I'm an awful person for the way I treated Sully."

"I went back looking for Sully. I wanted to apologize. I only found James. He told me Sully went home. He was so kind to me after what I'd done. He made me a cup of tea and listened while I cried and babbled hysterically."

"When he went to the back to get me tissues, I left. The poor guy has his own problems. He didn't need to take on mine. I finally drove home around 10 that night. As soon as I got in the door, I broke down and told Davis everything. He was angry but he hugged me and comforted me anyway."

Tabitha pauses and stares past me. She's going back to that night in her mind. I'm silent, so she can concentrate on that memory.

"I remember thinking how lucky I am to have such an understanding husband. Here, he thought I was out with my friends having a girls' night at the bar when I was really chastising and assaulting his best friend."

Against my better judgment, I interject my personal opinion, "I think what you did pales in comparison to the lies Davis told you about the business he was supposed to have sold." I want to say more but I bite my tongue. I could compromise this investigation by validating my suspect's conduct.

My comment causes Tabitha to snap back to reality. "I really don't think I should talk to you without a lawyer," she says as she inches toward the sidewalk leading to the front porch.

"Don't you think it's a little late for that?" I belittle and let out a laugh.

"My lawyer will be in touch," Tabitha sputters, failing to hide the fear in her voice.

As she turns to walk away, I call to her, "Just a friendly piece of advice, Mrs. Parks, you should send your kids to a relative."

Tabitha whirls back around and points at me. "You—" she growls. She stops herself and stomps dramatically up the porch steps and into her house.

After she's gone, I grin with satisfaction. Tabitha's fingerprint is on the tissue box in my car.

4 October 2013
(29 Years Old)

Schaumburg, Illinois

"I think I'm going to tell Ezra about us," Benny says casually.

Seconds before, we were talking and laughing and now, I have nothing to say. I look away from him, take a sip of my beer and set it down.

"That's not what you want, is it? For people to know we're seeing each other?" Benny breaks the awkward silence.

"It's a little soon, don't you think?" That's the best I can come up with.

"Three months is a long time for me. This is the longest relationship I've ever been in." He laughs.

"Relationship? This isn't really what I call a relationship. I mean, we don't even call or text. We just plan to meet here the same day and time each week," I argue.

"I know and I feel responsible for that. I didn't want anyone to know at first. I want that to change. I want to call you. I want to see you more. I want to stop acting like we hardly know each other at work. I don't want to pretend anymore."

"What if I don't want it to change?"

The tables are turned and this time, Benny doesn't know what to say.

"Why didn't you want anyone to know at first?" I ask. There's an edge to my tone, hinting that I already know the answer.

"Oh. Uh—" Benny slides a few inches away from me in the booth. I hear the cheap vinyl buckle underneath his weight. "The guys talk, you know? And uh, there are some rumors about your past. It's stupid. I know that now." His face and neck turn beet red.

"Why haven't you ever asked me if the rumors are true?" I realize I like watching him squirm and struggle to hold back a fiendish smile.

"The rumors don't matter. I just want to get to know you now, in the present." He chooses his next words carefully. "Just because your dad was committed, it doesn't mean you're—"

"Insane?" I finish.

"Exactly."

"You're too trusting. Most disorders are genetic. You know that, right?" I'm having a bit of fun with him.

"So, you're saying you are—" he's interrupted by his phone ringing. I see Ezra's name flash on the screen before Benny lifts his phone from the table. "Hold on. I need to take this."

I nod.

"Hey, bro! What's up?" Benny answers.

His volume is up so high, I can hear Ezra clearly.

"Where are you?" Ezra asks.

Benny looks at me and opens his mouth to speak. I sense he's going to confess, so I shake my head vigorously. He closes his mouth and blows air through his nostrils.

"I'm at home, man. Why? What's going on?" He recovers.

"No, you're not, bro. I already went by your apartment," Ezra huffs. "Where are you, for real?"

Benny clears his throat. "I'm home but I stepped out to get some beer from the corner store. You must've just missed me." He's talking in a slow, monotone voice. It's no surprise that Ezra doesn't believe him.

"Benny, cut the crap. You're in Schaumburg. What are you doing there?"

Benny mutes his phone and turns to me. "I forgot that I'm sharing my location with him."

"What? You're a grown man. Why do you have to share your location with anyone?" I'm trying to stay calm, but this is uncool.

"We were drunk one night and shared our locations with each other as a joke. What's the big deal anyway? This is our chance to come clean."

"Hello? Benny? Where'd you go?" Ezra demands.

Benny unmutes and looks at me pleadingly. I mouth the word 'no' and give him the death stare. "Sorry," he says to Ezra. "The TV was too loud. I had to turn it down."

"Stop trying to punk me, man. Who are you with? Why did you put me on mute?" Before Benny can answer, Ezra says, "You know what? Never mind. I'm coming in."

"Coming in?" It's too late. Ezra hangs up. Benny quickly checks Ezra's location and sees that he's right outside the restaurant.

Before Benny can stop me, I've slid down underneath the table and come out on the other side of the booth. I peer at the door and see Ezra pushing it open. I duck before he can see me.

"Please don't go," Benny begs.

I need to think fast. Say something to stop him from telling Ezra about me. "I'll come see you tomorrow night. At your apartment. After your shift," I entice.

"Really?" He responds in disbelief.

"Yes, really. Just don't tell Ezra about us yet. Promise?"

"Deal. He just spotted me. You should go that way." He points toward the exit door at the back of the restaurant.

Benny stands and walks toward Ezra to create a diversion. I speed walk with my back hunched over to the exit, fighting the temptation to look back. I made it this far without Ezra noticing me. I don't need to sabotage it by turning around.

I think the real reason Ezra didn't see me is because he wasn't looking for me. I'm the last person Ezra would expect to see on a date with his brother.

As I make a narrow escape out the back door, I catch a glimpse of Ezra sitting in the booth we were in. Luckily, his back is to me.

My beer mug still sits on the other side of the table next to Benny. I wonder how he's going to explain that one away. I'll never know what was said after I left. The following night, Benny was murdered in the alley next to his apartment building.

Present Day
12 October 2024

Sully's Read n Sip W. Madison St.

I can put out a warrant for Davis' arrest right now for lying to the police. I don't have enough on Tabitha yet. Slapping someone isn't grounds for murder charges.

The tissue box is in an evidence bag in my back seat. While I'm anxious to get the prints lifted, I need to talk to James again.

Since he left out the information about Sullivan's will and Tabitha returning to the shop that night, I have a feeling there's a couple more things he conveniently left out of his story.

When I enter *Sully's Read n Sip,* James is in his usual spot, behind the counter. I must've just missed the morning rush because there's only one person browsing the books at the far end of the store. James looks surprised to see me again.

"Are you going to keep the name?" I ask as I point to the lettering on the window, spelling *Sully's Read n Sip*.

"Uh, what do you mean?" James asks with a concerned expression.

"Since Sully left the shop to you, I'm just curious. Are you going to change the name?"

"I," sweat beads form on James' forehead, "don't think so. Wait. Did Davis tell you?"

"Yes and why didn't you?"

"It wasn't relevant." James wipes his forehead with a napkin.

"Why isn't it?"

"Because I didn't kill him," James whispers loudly. Loud enough for the one customer to look over at us.

"That's not what Davis thinks. You're protecting him and meanwhile, he's throwing you under the bus."

"I'm not protecting him. I don't even like that guy. I just need to stay in his good graces until he signs the rest of the company over to me."

"Did he agree to do that when he came to see you yesterday?"

"He's just telling all my business, huh?"

"Yes, so it's time for you to start telling his. I understand why you don't want to talk to me. He won't know where the information came from," I lie.

Tabitha has probably already told Davis that I came by yesterday, which means he'll know that James told me about the altercation. As far as I know, Davis hasn't called James about it yet, so I can still play the card that I haven't told Davis anything James told me about his wife.

James stands back, crosses his arms and frowns at me. I can tell this is going to take more coaxing than I anticipated.

"Look, how about I ask questions and you just answer with a yes or no? That way, you're not sharing any information that I don't already know. You're just confirming or denying."

"Alright. Sounds fair enough," James agrees with some skepticism.

"Did Tabitha come back to the shop looking for Sullivan about 20 minutes after the altercation?" I start out.

"Yes, but how—?"

I cut him off, "Tabitha was upset, beside herself, and was hoping to make amends with Sully."

"That's correct."

"You consoled her and offered her a cup of tea."

"It's scary how accurate you are. How do you know all this?"

"Around 8:45, you went to the back to grab a box of tissues for her and when you came back, she was gone."

"Yes, and the tea was gone, too." James claps his hand over his mouth. "I didn't mean to say that, but it was strange. It took me a few minutes to find a box of tissues and when I came back, she was gone along with the whole cup of tea. I mean, the cup and all."

"It wasn't a reusable cup," I seek clarification.

"No, it was a cup that we wash and reuse. Maybe she was such an emotional wreck that she didn't realize she was walking out with it. I've never had anyone do that before. That doesn't make her a murderer though," he quickly adds.

"Of course it doesn't, but that is certainly odd behavior," I agree.

"That's everything. You've got all the information I have. After she left, that was the last I've seen of her."

"I believe that. Is there anything you want to share about your visit with Davis yesterday?"

"He cried. As soon as he walked in here, he broke down. He's heartbroken over the loss of his friend. I know you have a job to do, Detective, but we're all grieving here. Can you let up just a little to let us grieve?"

"That's not how it works, James. The more days that pass, the colder the trail becomes. Do you want this to become a cold case?"

"No, not at all."

"Then you need to cooperate. If you come across any new information, you need to share it with me immediately. Otherwise, you'll be arrested for impeding an investigation."

James' eyes widen. If I didn't have his attention before, I've got it now.

"Understood. I'll let you know if I learn any new information. Please believe me when I say that there isn't anything new I can share with you right now."

I believe him. James gives me a free cup of coffee in a to-go cup. I can't help but think he gave it to me more out of fear than out of kindness. He must think that if he's kind to me, I won't arrest him. That's comical.

I didn't record this conversation because I know my unconventional means of interrogation may be looked down upon by the bureau. Submitting another recorded interview wasn't the purpose of this visit anyway. The purpose was to confirm that Tabitha has no alibi from 8:45–10 that night.

14 October 2013
(29 Years Old)

My Apartment N. Clark St.

I didn't attend Benny's memorial service. It's in my best interests that no one knows about how close we were. I'm a little freaked out by the fact that I'm not bothered by his death.

When I look in the mirror, I don't recognize myself. I can't stare for longer than a few seconds without turning away, ashamed of what I've become. I try to force tears from my eyes but they remain dry as a desert.

I'm a heartless monster. Incapable of attachment. Just like my dad. In all fairness, I tried to warn Benny that I'm damaged. The other night at the restaurant, I wasn't joking when I said insanity can be an inherited trait.

I close my eyes and try to imagine an alternate reality. A reality where I had a normal relationship with Benny. Where we fell madly in love and introduced each other to our families.

My daydream quickly takes a turn when I imagine him cheating on me and then abusing me. He makes it seem like it's my fault that he cheated. He convinces me that I asked for the abuse by questioning him or running my mouth.

I open my eyes and feel validated for not caring that he's gone.

Present Day
12 October 2024

Bureau of Detectives, Forensic Services Division

"Run this print against the print on the mug," I say, as I lay the transparent tape with the print I lifted from the tissue box on Ezra's desk.

"Whose print is this?" Ezra looks up from his paperwork.

"Tabitha Parks," I say in a way that suggests he should know who it belongs to.

"We're stealing prints from unsuspecting people now?"

"I have probable cause to believe that she's responsible for the murder of Sullivan Maxwell. That makes her a suspect, not just some random person. Once this print matches the one on the mug, that will make her a criminal."

"Sullivan may have invited her over for a cup of coffee. That doesn't make her a criminal," he reasons.

"We'll see about that. Just run the prints." Ezra stares up at me until I add, "Please."

"Whatever you say, boss." Ezra grabs the print and heads to the lab.

I head to my office to catch up on emails and paperwork as I wait for the results. An hour later, there's a knock on the door. It's Ezra.

"It's a perfect match. The print on the mug matches the print you provided. That's what you want to hear, right? It still doesn't prove that Tabitha murdered Sullivan. Now what?"

"You'll see. Come with me to the Parks' house and be prepared to make an arrest," I say as I stand to gather my belongings.

"That won't be necessary," Ezra stops me. "Tabitha Parks is here. Waiting to speak to you."

"Well, isn't that convenient? Her guilty conscience must've gotten to her. Send her in." I sit back down.

This time, I take out my recorder and press record before Tabitha comes in. I stand to greet her and reach out to shake her hand. She refuses to shake mine, so I point to a chair for her to sit in across from me. Ezra closes the door and leans against it. I gesture for him to sit but he shakes his head.

"What brings you to us, Tabitha?" I begin.

Tabitha is shaking and her eyes are red and swollen.

"I know you're not going to stop until you arrest me. You've already made up your mind that I'm guilty. I don't want my kids to watch their mom get dragged away in handcuffs. Davis and I talked and he's hired a lawyer to defend me. So, arrest me now and my lawyer will get me out later."

"Are you confessing to the murder of Sullivan Maxwell?" I lean closer to the microphone.

"No, I'm not confessing." She shakes her head and looks around at me and then at Ezra. "I'm cooperating so my family is left alone."

"Since you're willing to cooperate, tell us about the night of October 5th."

Tabitha sniffles and takes a deep breath. "I need to go back a little further before I can explain my actions that night. May I have a drink of water please?" She directs the question to Ezra, knowing he'll take pity on her.

Being the gentleman that he is, he leaves to grab her a bottled water from the breakroom. Tabitha and I avoid eye contact while he's gone. When Ezra returns, he opens the bottle before handing it to her.

"You've got to be kidding me," I say under my breath.

She can't open her own water.

Ezra shrugs his shoulders and resumes his position by leaning on the closed door. He looks smug like he's enjoying this delay. It's apparent that he still isn't supporting me on this.

Tabitha takes a few gulps of the water and replaces the cap.

Can we get on with it? I'm screaming internally.

"The day before," Tabitha begins again.

"October 4th?" I interrupt.

"Yes, on October 4th, I received a phone call from the loan company. Not my loan company. The company that holds the loan for *Sully's Read n Sip*. At first, they didn't want to talk to me. They only wanted to talk to Davis, but I argued that I'm his wife and handle our finances."

"The person I spoke with gave in and told me that Sullivan was four months behind in payments. They made multiple failed attempts to reach him, so they were seeking payment from Davis. I was floored. Davis's name wasn't even supposed to be on the loan. He promised to get out in 2017 before we got married. I don't know why he thought I'd never find out."

"Did you confront Davis when he got home that day?" I ask.

"No. Believe me, I was livid. I think he could sense something was up, but I wasn't ready to say anything yet."

"That doesn't make sense. Why wouldn't you want to confront him immediately?" I chastise. Ezra flashes me a look of disapproval. He's not wrong. I don't want to be accused of antagonizing the suspect.

"Davis is the breadwinner. He did what he told me he would do which is provide for our family. I was angry but didn't want this to destroy us. I decided to give myself time to calm down before I talked to him. Then, we could approach this problem together."

More like you didn't want to leave him and let go of the lavish lifestyle he provides for you.

"The news only got worse, didn't it?" I try to sound sympathetic. Ezra looks elsewhere and covers his mouth with his hand, so I don't see him fighting back a smile. We both know how fake I sound.

Tabitha ignores us and answers my question, "Yes, the afternoon of October 5th, I went out to get the mail and there was a letter from the IRS addressed to Davis. I really do handle our finances, so I opened it without him."

"The letter stated that Sullivan and Davis owe taxes on *Sully's Read n Sip*. Not just a small amount but they owe two years of back taxes. That was the last straw."

"The person I really wanted to face was Sullivan. In my mind, he was responsible for all of this. It was his business, his loan, his back taxes that turned our lives upside down."

"When Davis got home from work, I told him I had plans with some friends. I don't get out much, so he's really good about handling the kids so I can have a life. Lying to him made me sick."

"Not sick enough to back out," I realize I said that out loud. Tabitha glares at me and Ezra flashes me another look to tone it down. I'm allowing my impatience to get the best of me.

"I suppose you have a point. I wasn't sick enough to back out. That night, I drove to *Sully's Read n Sip*. When I arrived around 8, James and Sullivan were talking and shelving books."

"Just seeing him so relaxed, without a care in the world, infuriated me. I lost my temper. My plan to have a civilized conversation and ask him to handle the mess he put us in went out the window."

"I was yelling and carrying on about the lies, the loan payments, and the back taxes. I'm mortified about the way I behaved. I made James feel so uneasy that he hid behind a bookcase. He heard everything though. I know he did."

"They were closing soon, so fortunately, there weren't any customers. Sullivan still convinced me to go outside. I followed him for James' sake."

"We stood on the sidewalk, right outside the store window, and everything I wanted to say came out as a yell. I couldn't help it. I couldn't understand why he was so calm after what he'd done to us."

"I feel awful talking about him like this since he's deceased, but you have to understand why I lost my temper with him. When I didn't think I could be pushed any further, he said something that sent me reeling."

"He said this was my fault for forcing Davis to abandon the business. Davis was the brains and Sullivan the visionary. He claimed the business wouldn't be failing if Davis were still in it."

"I snapped and slapped him across the face. I have really long nails, so I'm pretty sure I scratched him by accident. After that, there was nothing left to say. I stormed off to my car and well, Sullivan was left there, holding his cheek. That's the last time I saw him."

Tabitha takes a sip of water and stares past me. I wonder if she's going to talk about what happened after the altercation, so I give her time to gather her thoughts but she's mute.

"Did you try calling him or contacting him after that?" I press.

"I'm sorry but this is all my lawyer permitted me to say. Everything after this point is your word against mine. The rest of the story will have to wait to be told in front of a judge."

"I understand. I have one more question though. I'm sure your lawyer won't mind you answering this one. Have you ever been inside Sullivan's apartment?"

"I suppose it won't hurt for me to answer that. No, I have not. I've never had a reason to. See? That should help my defense. How could I murder a man inside an apartment that I've never been to?" Tabitha lets out a sigh of relief like she's just won her own case.

I look at Ezra, but he refuses to look at me. He knows Tabitha just gave me probable cause to arrest her. Prima facie once again!

"Your fingerprint was found on a mug in Sullivan's apartment. How do you explain that, Mrs. Parks?" *Finally! I've been waiting this whole agonizing interview to be able to say that.*

Tabitha's jaw drops and there's a wild look in her eyes. "What are you talking about? I've been framed! I want my lawyer," she panics.

"That's not a problem. We'll let you contact your lawyer. In the meantime, you're under arrest."

I open my desk drawer and grab a pair of handcuffs. As I walk around the desk, Tabitha melts into a bawling mess on the floor. She refuses to stand and when I look to Ezra for assistance, he stays put and watches.

That's fine. I'll handle this one on my own.

I forcefully yank Tabitha to her feet and pull both of her hands behind her back to cuff her. As I read the Miranda Warning, she's screaming and putting on a real spectacle, swinging her body and knocking things off my desk. I call for backup on my walkie.

Ezra opens the door to allow me to lead her out. Within minutes, two officers meet me outside my office and I turn

Tabitha over to them. After her cries taper off, I walk coolly back into my office and push stop on the recorder.

Ezra and I face off.

"Why did you do that?" I exclaim.

"I told you Tabitha Parks is innocent," Ezra replies calmly.

"You heard her. She lied and said she's never been in Sullivan's apartment," I contend.

"It sounds like she's been framed," Ezra says as he runs a hand nonchalantly through his hair.

You smug prick.

"I could have you suspended," I threaten.
"But you won't." He smirks.

10 March 2014
(30 Years Old)

The Bean Chicago, Illinois

"This is really how you want to celebrate your birthday? Looking at a giant bean in the freezing cold?" Ezra brings his gloved hands to his face and blows into them.

"You grew up here, you big baby. You should be able to handle colder weather than this," I push him in a teasing way.

It really is cold out here. A few degrees colder and our breath might freeze mid-air.

"Just a few more minutes and then we can go someplace warm," I beg.

Ezra laughs. "Alright. If I can put up with you, then I can put up with anything."

"Exactly how I feel about you," I reply charmingly.

"Tell me the story," Ezra prompts.

As I'm looking up at the Bean, I say, "What do you mean?"

"What makes this spot special to you?" He elaborates.

"Oh, the few times my dad brought me and Farah with him to Chicago, he left us here while he went out and looked for work." I put 'looked for work' in air quotes.

"He left you here? For how long?" Ezra sounds concerned.

I laugh to take the edge off the conversation. "Only for a few hours and it was just a day trip. It wasn't like he left us overnight or anything."

"When you say looked for work, do you mean—?" He pauses.

I say what he's struggling to say, "He got hammered at a bar while we played at the Bean."

"Oh, Mila. I'm so sorry." I cringe at the pity in his tone. I don't even want to see what kind of look he's giving me but I feel his eyes burning into the side of my face.

"Like I've said, not everyone gets to have a happy childhood." I keep my gaze fixed on the Bean.

"Thank you," Ezra says.

Now, I do look at him. We joke around so much, I don't know if he's being sincere or sarcastic.

"For what?" I ask.

"For making the last several months bearable."

"You should thank the Chief for forcing you to be my partner," I joke.

"Seriously, Mila. After Benny's—" he can't say it and I don't make him finish. "I didn't want to live any longer. I didn't see the point in any of it. While you'll never be him—"

"Geez, thanks," I pretend to be offended.

"You know what I mean. You can't replace him and he can't replace you. You've played different roles in my life."

"I was only kidding. I know what you mean. You'll never replace Farah, but it doesn't make you less important."

"Exactly. So, you do understand what I'm trying to say." Ezra's relieved that we're on the same page.

I smile reassuringly. That's when he leans in and his warm, soft lips connect with mine. I don't pull away even though everything inside of me is telling me to. Instead, I go with it.

This is the first time I've felt something, other than disgust or regret, during a kiss. It scares me how different it feels. I'm eventually the one to pull away. Ezra reads my expression. I'm more distraught than elated.

"I know what you're thinking," he says. "We're partners."

"This will never work," we say in unison.

"But I say it will," he asserts. I admire his charisma. He goes on, "I'll transfer to another precinct just for you to give this a chance."

"Ezra, there are so many things you don't know about me. If you only knew—"

"Then, give me a chance to get to know you and make that decision for myself," he persuades.

"No," I say firmly.

"What?" He's taken aback. His optimism fades.

"No, I just want to be partners and friends right now, in that order," I say without an ounce of uncertainty in my voice.

"Oh. Okay. If that's how you truly feel, then I'll respect that," he responds dispiritedly.

"Honestly?" I'm expecting an argument and here he is being reasonable.

"Yes, what kind of man would I be if I didn't respect a woman's wishes? I'd be a real jerk." He shoves his hands in his coat pockets and looks up at the Bean.

I stare at him for a few seconds. I haven't met a man like him before. He's a real gentleman. I wish I had gotten to know him sooner. Maybe if I had, things would've been different.

Present Day
12 October 2024

My Apartment N. Clark St.

I'm relaxing on the love seat in my living room with a glass of Chardonnay. My apartment is dark and silent as I stare out the picture window at the night sky. It's a cloudless night and I'm mapping the constellations with my eyes.

There's a knock at my door. I'm not expecting any visitors at this late hour. I flick on the light and look through the peephole to see Ezra standing outside my door. He's alone but this is unusual for him to show up unannounced.

"Hey, what's going on?" I ask suspiciously as I'm opening the door.

"Can I come in?" He asks when he's already halfway through my doorway.

I step aside and allow him to pass me.

"By all means, make yourself at home," I reply with a hint of sarcasm.

He walks to the middle of the living room and stares out at the night sky. The same night sky I was admiring before his intrusion. I'm annoyed that he's impeding on my quiet time.

"Ezra, can I help you?" I close the door and walk over, stopping beside him. When he doesn't answer, I add, "Can I get you anything? Water? Wine? Beer?"

"No thank you, *Natalia,*" he says casually while still looking out the window.

"What did you just call me?"

"You heard me. *Natalia,*" he hisses.

"Ezra, that's not my name. Are you feeling ok?"

He turns to look at me this time. His eyes are like a dark void. "I know that's not your name, but it is a name you've gone by before."

"I don't understand. Where is this coming from?" I'm searching his eyes for any sign that this is just a practical joke but his eyes remain stone cold. *He's serious.*

"You can stop the act. I've known for some time now. I've just been gathering evidence and biding my time." I'm silent but continuing to maintain eye contact so he continues, "I was never able to accept that Deek was Benny's killer. You know that."

"The part you don't know is even after he was sentenced, I kept investigating. Sometimes, I wish I hadn't because what I uncovered gives me nightmares."

I cross my arms and arrogantly urge him, "Go on."

"I believed Deek when he said he was set up and the wallet was planted outside his apartment for him to find. I believe that he never met Benny and had nothing to do with his murder. I may never be able to prove it though. The trail was too cold by then."

I smirk.

"I know you were seeing him. That's how I know you're guilty. An innocent person wouldn't hide her relationship with the victim. The night I crashed your date, I took fingerprints and a DNA sample from the beer mug you left behind."

"I've known it was you for so long. At first, I convinced myself that someday, you would tell me about your relationship with him. I told myself that you were scared about how it looked, so that's why you hadn't told me yet. The closer I got to you, the more evident it became that you were never going to tell me."

I look away, telling him everything he needs to know.

"I started following you. That New Year's Eve in 2016, I didn't really leave. I came back in through the back entrance and hid in a booth. You met Sullivan in the pub that night but that wasn't the last time you saw him, was it?"

"You sought him out years later. You hadn't solved a big case since Benny's, so you needed him. You needed his death, his murder, to guarantee your promotion to Deputy Ch—"

"You're just talking nonsense," I cut him off. "I can't believe you've been spying on me. All these years, I thought you were the one person I could trust." My mind is racing but I keep my cool. *Don't give away anything he doesn't already know.*

"I have photos, Mila. I have photos of you with Sullivan. Don't you think it looks suspicious that you knew him, had some kind of relationship with him, and you've been investigating his death like he was a stranger?"

My face feels flushed. *Was I really that sloppy?* Arrogance really does lead to one's downfall.

Not waiting for a response, he goes on, "I also have a witness. Sullivan's neighbor, Mr. Brewer, I went to see him about a week after he returned from visiting his son. He was pretty shaken up but not because of Sullivan's death."

"He kept raving on about how much you look like Natalia, the woman he saw in Sullivan's apartment. He told me about his encounter with you earlier that week. He's certain that you weren't there to investigate a crime but to make sure you'd covered your tracks."

I knew I should've taken care of that old man.

"It doesn't sound like an open and shut case to me," I make a cynical observation.

"It isn't but I do have a prima facie case." He follows with a sinister smile and holds up two small plastic bags. "You see, I can hide things from you, too. When I investigated the crime scene, the morning Sullivan's body was found, I found this on the fire escape outside of his apartment."

He holds one of the plastic bags a little higher. "A dark strand of synthetic hair. The other day, in Sycamore, when I tried on your wig, I snatched this." He raises the other bag. "The strand I found on Sully's fire escape and the strand I took from your wig are an exact match. Try to explain that to a judge."

I have to admit that I'm impressed. *Ezra is a better detective than I ever gave him credit for.*

"How'd you convince him to allow you to enter through the fire escape? Off the record, what do you say to a man to convince him to allow you to do such a crazy thing?"

I believe him when he says he's asking me off the record. Besides, I've been a detective long enough to know that with the photos and the strands of hair, he has enough evidence to arrest me. Maybe not to convict, but enough to go to trial.

Above all, I consider answering his question because I'm taking pleasure in the fact that he has to ask. He wasn't able to figure out that detail on his own and he needs my help to make sense of it.

"You'll get a kick out of this. I told him that my abusive ex-husband was stalking me. I claimed he was a detective named Ezra Wilkins. I convinced him that our relationship had to be kept a secret, otherwise my life would be in danger." I wait for Ezra to acknowledge my genius but instead, he looks horrified.

"How'd you manage to get Tabitha's fingerprint planted on the mug?"

"Let's just say a teacup was involved." I shrug.

"Never mind. I don't think I can handle any more details anyway." He holds up a hand, letting me know that he doesn't want me to elaborate.

I've rendered him speechless, so I change the subject. "The day we went to Sycamore, when we stopped at my old house, did you know?"

Ezra remains quiet for a moment, still struggling to process the bomb I dropped on him. I'm beginning to think he isn't going to answer when he says, "That Farah lives there? Yes. I wanted to see how far you were willing to go to keep up with the lies you told."

"I didn't just follow you. I dug deep into your past. I visited the Chester Mental Institution. With your dad being deceased, the staff handed over his file without hesitation.

It gave me an odd sense of relief to find out that most of what you told me about that day was true."

"Most, but not all. You conveniently left out how Farah was in a coma, not dead, and she woke up after four months. I found records of Farah's visits to your dad at Chester and transcripts of his conversations with the psychiatrists on staff where he detailed the incident. He said he *nearly* killed his daughter. Why would you lie about your sister dying? What did you gain from that?"

I shrug. "The narrative of the detective who witnessed the *near* death of her sister doesn't gain as much sympathy as the narrative of the detective who witnessed her sister's death."

Ezra stares at me blankly. I know a million thoughts are racing through his mind. I can see him trying to make sense of it all. I break his concentration by asking, "So, what now, Ezra?"

"You're going to jail, Mila. You're not the only one who can build a solid case against someone based on how a situation appears. Do you have an alibi for the night Sullivan was murdered? What about Benny?" Ezra searches my face for any sign of remorse. I remain stoic and silent.

It's apparent that he isn't going to get what he truly wants from me, which is a confession to both murders, so he moves on, "I have some guys outside waiting to come in and arrest you. I came in here unarmed and without a wire because I wanted to prove to myself that I can look Benny's killer in the eye and use restraint. I also think I deserve answers."

Suddenly, his posture and tone shift from aggressive to defeated and pathetic. "Please," he appeals to our relationship, "if you ever loved me at all, do this for me. Explain this to me, so I can try to understand."

A wave of pity for him overcomes me. "I did love you at one time." I pause to release a deep breath. "But," I pause again, "I'm incapable of feeling any real attachment to anyone. These weren't crimes of passion. I needed a way to move up in a system overrun by men. That's all."

"Wow." He shakes his head and clenches his fists as his body tenses up. "You really are insane. I don't know why I thought hearing your explanation, or whatever that was, would lessen the pain, make the knife dug into my back a little duller."

Ezra is trembling with anger. If he didn't have guys outside, I think he'd strangle me with his bare hands right now. "No, listening to you talk makes me wonder how I ever loved you. How I can still care for you now. Would I have been your next victim?"

I look away again. I would never hurt him. I couldn't. I don't bother to tell him because he won't believe me and for good reason.

He must recognize that he's on the verge of losing control because he calls for his guys to come in. Ezra stands back with an eerie look of satisfaction as one of the guys grabs me and pushes me up against the wall. As he cuffs me and pats me down for weapons, the other guy reads me my rights.

While being led out of my apartment, I look back to see Ezra looking down at the coffee table where he must've noticed one of the letters from my dad. I know which letter it is. I read it almost every night. I can practically recite it by heart.

9 March 2003

Dear Mila,

A memory from your childhood keeps playing over and over in my mind. You were eight years old and Farah was babysitting you after school while I was at work. When I came home, a window in the living room was broken and one of Farah's softballs was in the yard.

Her bat was lying near the window inside. You met me in the driveway and told me frantically that you tried to stop her, but Farah was playing softball in the house when she hit the ball too hard and busted the window.

I went in to find Farah sleeping in her bed with headphones on. I argued with her about the window. She denied having anything to do with it and said she'd been sleeping since she got home from school. I believed her but I never told you that.

This was one of many stories I can tell you. I have so many stories to share of when you manipulated a situation to appear as you wanted it to be. I plan to tell you all of them through these letters.

I know you'll remember every story I tell but I want to make you aware that I know you were trying to deceive me. I didn't recognize it as deception at the time and I wish I had. Things would've been so different for us if I had gotten the help I needed.

It's too late for me now but if I can help you see the things I didn't, then maybe you can save yourself. Maybe you can get the help I was never able to give you.

I was a bad father in more ways than one. I saw how you set your sister up to take the fall for your mistakes time after time and I let you get away with it. At the time, I thought the way you framed your sister was ingenious.

I saw it as a sign of strength and intelligence. While your eight-year-old mind wasn't quite capable of outsmarting an adult yet, I knew your intelligence would surpass mine someday.

I recognize now that your plots and schemes were a way for you to receive positive attention from me. I never gave you what you were yearning for. I did the opposite of what you wanted. I continued to ignore you, leaving you feeling disappointed and neglected.

As I said before, I let you get away with it back then but that's not what a good father would do. A good father would've sat you down and taught you right from wrong. A good father would've taught you how to channel that intelligence and cunning into something positive.

I was sick and didn't recognize it. Until that horrific day, my illness didn't allow me to recognize the mental illness in you.

When I witnessed how far you were willing to go for my approval, I blamed myself for what you had become and took the fall for you.

The moment you came out of nowhere and smashed the bottle across your poor sister's head during my argument with her, I became terrified and knew my presence in your life was only driving a wedge of hatred and jealousy between you and Farah.

Don't, for one second, have pity on me though. Rather, take full advantage of the second chance I've given you. Repair your relationship with Farah. Your sister loves you and can care for you better than I ever could, Mila. She is as kind and compassionate as your mother.

I'll leave you with these final words. I hope you've recognized the darkness within you and learned to overcome it. I hope you've achieved success by making an honest living. Forgive me for not being the one to point you in the right direction.

Love,

Dad